William Shakespeare's
As You Like It
In Plain and Simple English

BOOKCAPS

A SwipeSpeare™ Book
www.SwipeSpeare.com

About This Series

The "SwipeSpeare™" series started as a way of telling Shakespeare for the modern reader—being careful to preserve the themes and integrity of the original. Visit our website SwipeSpeare.com to see other books in the series, as well as the interactive, and swipe-able, app!

The series is expanding every month. Visit BookCaps.com to see non-Shakespeare books in this series, and while you are there join the Facebook page, so you are first to know when a new book comes out.

Characters

DUKE, living in exile

FREDERICK, Brother to the Duke, and Usurper of his Dominions

AMIENS, Lord attending on the Duke in his Banishment

JAQUES, Lord attending on the Duke in his Banishment

LE BEAU, a Courtier attending upon Frederick

CHARLES, his Wrestler

OLIVER, Son of Sir Rowland de Bois

JAQUES, Son of Sir Rowland de Bois

ORLANDO, Son of Sir Rowland de Bois

ADAM, Servant to Oliver

DENNIS, Servant to Oliver

TOUCHSTONE, a Clown

SIR OLIVER MARTEXT, a Vicar

CORIN, Shepherd

SILVIUS, Shepherd

WILLIAM, a Country Fellow, in love with Audrey.

A person representing HYMEN.

ROSALIND, Daughter to the banished Duke

CELIA, Daughter to Frederick

PHEBE, a Shepherdess

AUDREY, a Country Wench

Lords belonging to the two Dukes; Pages, Foresters, and other Attendants.

Play

Act I

SCENE I. Orchard of Oliver's house.

Enter ORLANDO and ADAM

ORLANDO

As I remember, Adam, it was upon this fashion bequeathed me by will but poor a thousand crowns,
and, as thou sayest, charged my brother, on his blessing, to breed me well: and there begins my sadness. My brother Jaques he keeps at school, and
report speaks goldenly of his profit: for my part, he keeps me rustically at home, or, to speak more
properly, stays me here at home unkept; for call you
that keeping for a gentleman of my birth, that differs not from the stalling of an ox? His horses are bred better; for, besides that they are fair with their feeding, they are taught their manage, and to that end riders dearly hired: but I, his brother, gain nothing under him but growth; for the
which his animals on his dunghills are as much bound to him as I. Besides this nothing that he so
plentifully gives me, the something that nature gave
me his countenance seems to take from me: he lets
me feed with his hinds, bars me the place of a brother, and, as much as in him lies, mines my gentility with my education. This is it, Adam, that
grieves me; and the spirit of my father, which I think is within me, begins to mutiny against this servitude: I will no longer endure it, though yet I know no wise remedy how to avoid it.

ADAM

Yonder comes my master, your brother.

ORLANDO

Go apart, Adam, and thou shalt hear how he will

Adam, I remember that this was why my father left me only a thousand crowns in his will and, like you said, tasked my brother, while blessing him, to raise me. This began my sad problems. My brother, Oliver, keeps my other brother, Jacques, at school, where everyone says he is doing very well, but me he keeps here at home in the country, or to be more exact, cages me here. Do you think that it is fitting for such a noble man as me to be in the same situation as an ox? Oliver's horses are treated better than me: they are fed well and they are trained by well paid trainers. Meanwhile, I, his own brother, get nothing from his care, unless you count growing and maturing naturally – his animals, sitting on piles of dung and manure, get as much from him and are just as tied to him. He gives me a lot of nothing, and even my noble birthrights he has taken away from me: he makes me eat with his servants, doesn't let me have what is rightfully mine as his brother, and, as much as he can, ruins my upbringing by refusing me a proper education. This, Adam, is why I am sad. My father's spirit – and I think I share his independence – begs me to rebel against this servanthood. I will stand for this no longer, even though I am not sure how to put a stop to it.

Here comes your brother, my master.

Go hide, Adam, and you will hear how

shake me up.

poorly he treats me.

Enter OLIVER

OLIVER
Now, sir! what make you here?

Hello, you! What are you doing here?

ORLANDO
Nothing: I am not taught to make any thing.

Nothing – I was never taught how to do anything.

OLIVER
What mar you then, sir?

Then what are you destroying?

ORLANDO
Marry, sir, I am helping you to mar that which God
made, a poor unworthy brother of yours, with
idleness.

Well, I am destroying that which God made – your brother who has nothing to do.

OLIVER
Marry, sir, be better employed, and be naught
awhile.

Then you should find something to do and go away for a while.

ORLANDO
Shall I keep your hogs and eat husks with them?
What prodigal portion have I spent, that I should
come to such penury?

Would you like me to watch your pigs and eat their food with them? When did I act like the prodigal son and spend my inheritance, so that I must be punished like this?

OLIVER
Know you where your are, sir?

Do you know where you are?

ORLANDO
O, sir, very well; here in your orchard.

Yes, I am in your orchard,

OLIVER
Know you before whom, sir?

And do you know who you are talking to?

ORLANDO
Ay, better than him I am before knows me. I know
you are my eldest brother; and, in the gentle
condition of blood, you should so know me. The
courtesy of nations allows you my better, in that
you are the first-born; but the same tradition
takes not away my blood, were there twenty
brothers

Yes, I know him better than he knows me. I know you are my oldest brother, and I know you are a gentleman by birth, but you should know that I am too. General tradition says that you are my elder and should be respected, since you are first-born, but that same tradition does not take away my nobility, even if there were twenty brothers and I was the youngest. I have just as

betwixt us: I have as much of my father in me as you; albeit, I confess, your coming before me is nearer to his reverence.

even if, I admit, your place as being born first much of my father's blood in me as you do – was more honored by him.

OLIVER
What, boy!

How dare you!

strikes ORLANDO

ORLANDO
Come, come, elder brother, you are too young in this.

Now, now – you may be my older brother, but you are not very experienced in fighting.

seizes OLIVER

OLIVER
Wilt thou lay hands on me, villain?

Do you dare touch me, scoundrel?

ORLANDO
I am no villain; I am the youngest son of Sir Rowland de Boys; he was my father, and he is thrice
a villain that says such a father begot villains.
Wert thou not my brother, I would not take this hand
from thy throat till this other had pulled out thy tongue for saying so: thou hast railed on thyself.

I am not a scoundrel: I am the youngest son of Sir Rowland de Boys. He is my father, and whoever says that he had scoundrels as sons is himself three times the scoundrel.
If you were not my brother, I would keep choking you with this hand while my other one would rip out your tongue for suggesting such a thing. You have insulted only yourself.

ADAM
Sweet masters, be patient: for your father's remembrance, be at accord.

Masters, please stop. For your father's sake, be at peace.

OLIVER
Let me go, I say.

Let me go, now.

ORLANDO
I will not, till I please: you shall hear me. My father charged you in his will to give me good education: you have trained me like a peasant, obscuring and hiding from me all gentleman-like
qualities. The spirit of my father grows strong in me, and I will no longer endure it: therefore allow
me such exercises as may become a gentleman, or
give me the poor allottery my father left me by testament; with that I will go buy my fortunes.

Not until I want to – first you will listen. My father requested in his will that you make sure I get a good education, and yet you have had me educated like a peasant and commoner, failing to teach me the proper qualities of a gentleman. I have the same character of my father in me and so I will no longer stand for this treatment. Either train me in the proper ways of becoming a gentleman or
give me the small inheritance that my father let me in his will, and I will leave to pursue my own future.

OLIVER

And what wilt thou do? beg, when that is spent?
Well, sir, get you in: I will not long be troubled
with you; you shall have some part of your will:
I
pray you, leave me.

And then what will you do? Will you beg from
me when you run out of money? Well, fine, get –
I will not be bothered by you any longer. You
will have your inheritance and then,
please, leave.

ORLANDO

I will no further offend you than becomes me
for my good.

I will not bother you any more than I have to so
that I get what is due me.

OLIVER

Get you with him, you old dog.

Go away with him, you old dog.

ADAM

Is 'old dog' my reward? Most true, I have lost
my
teeth in your service. God be with my old
master!
he would not have spoke such a word.

An 'old dog' am I? True enough – I am old
enough to have lost my teeth serving you and
your family. God be with your father,
my old master! He would never have called me
such a name.

Exeunt ORLANDO and ADAM

OLIVER

Is it even so? begin you to grow upon me? I will
physic your rankness, and yet give no thousand
crowns neither. Holla, Dennis!

Is it true? Have you grown big enough to
challenge me? Well, I will cure your rashness
against me and will not give you a thousand
crowns either. Hello, Dennis!

Enter DENNIS

DENNIS

Calls your worship?

You called, your worship?

OLIVER

Was not Charles, the duke's wrestler, here to
speak with me?

Has the duke's wrestler, Charles, come to see
me yet?

DENNIS

So please you, he is here at the door and
importunes
access to you.

He is in fact here at the door now, and asks
to speak with you.

OLIVER

Call him in.

Call him in.

Exit DENNIS

'Twill be a good way; and to-morrow the wrestling is.

This will work – and, tomorrow is the wrestling match.

Enter CHARLES

CHARLES
Good morrow to your worship.

Hello, your worship.

OLIVER
Good Monsieur Charles, what's the new news at the
new court?

Good sir Charles, what is the news at the new court?

CHARLES
There's no news at the court, sir, but the old news:
that is, the old duke is banished by his younger
brother the new duke; and three or four loving lords
have put themselves into voluntary exile with him,
whose lands and revenues enrich the new duke;
therefore he gives them good leave to wander.

Only the old news, sir:
that the duke has been banished by his younger
brother who has become the new duke, and
three or four devoted lords
have joined the old duke in voluntary exile –
but since their land and money have been given up to the new duke,
he has freely allowed them to leave.

OLIVER
Can you tell if Rosalind, the duke's daughter, be
banished with her father?

Was Rosalind, the old duke's daughter,
banished with her father?

CHARLES
O, no; for the duke's daughter, her cousin, so loves
her, being ever from their cradles bred together,
that she would have followed her exile, or have died
to stay behind her. She is at the court, and no
less beloved of her uncle than his own daughter; and
never two ladies loved as they do.

No, the new duke's daughter, Rosalind's cousin, loves
her – they were raised together from their
cradles – and would have followed her into
exile or would have died
without her. Rosalind is at the court, and she
is just as loved by her uncle as his own
daughter, Celia. Two ladies were never so fond
of each other as they are.

OLIVER
Where will the old duke live?

Where will the old duke live?

CHARLES
They say he is already in the forest of Arden, and
a many merry men with him; and there they live like

Some say he is already in the forest of Arden
with a group of happy men, living like
Robin Hood from England. They say young
gentleman come to him every day and spend the

the old Robin Hood of England: they say many young
gentlemen flock to him every day, and fleet the time
carelessly, as they did in the golden world.

time
without a care in the world, as if it were the Garden of Eden.

OLIVER
What, you wrestle to-morrow before the new duke?

So will you be wrestling tomorrow in front of the new duke?

CHARLES
Marry, do I, sir; and I came to acquaint you with a
matter. I am given, sir, secretly to understand
that your younger brother Orlando hath a disposition
to come in disguised against me to try a fall.
To-morrow, sir, I wrestle for my credit; and he that
escapes me without some broken limb shall acquit him
well. Your brother is but young and tender; and,
for your love, I would be loath to foil him, as I
must, for my own honour, if he come in: therefore,
out of my love to you, I came hither to acquaint you
withal, that either you might stay him from his
intendment or brook such disgrace well as he shall
run into, in that it is a thing of his own search
and altogether against my will.

Yes, sir, I will be – and I have come to talk with you
about a relevant problem. I was secretly informed
that your younger brother, Orlando, is planning
to fight against me in a disguise.
Tomorrow, sir, I am fighting to show off, so anyone
who escapes without a broken bone is lucky.
Your brother is young and weak still, and,
out of my love for you, I would feel bad if I destroyed him,
as I must in order to win the honor I am looking to win. So,
since I admire you, I came to tell you
so that you can either force him away from this
plan or can prepare him for the disgrace
he will face in fighting me – disgrace that will be his fault
and not something I am looking forward to.

OLIVER
Charles, I thank thee for thy love to me, which
thou shalt find I will most kindly requite. I had
myself notice of my brother's purpose herein and
have by underhand means laboured to dissuade him from
it, but he is resolute. I'll tell thee, Charles:
it is the stubbornest young fellow of France, full
of ambition, an envious emulator of every man's
good parts, a secret and villanous contriver against

Charles, thank you for your respect and loyalty,
which I will certainly reward you for. I
discovered my brother's intentions and
have subtly tried to persuade him against
it, but he is determined to go through with it. I
will tell you, Charles,
that Orlando is one of the most stubborn men in France, very
ambitious, and also very jealous of every man's
good qualities. Also, he is a cunning and
villainous liar who schemes

me his natural brother: therefore use thy
discretion; I had as lief thou didst break his neck
as his finger. And thou wert best look to't; for if
thou dost him any slight disgrace or if he do not
mightily grace himself on thee, he will practise
against thee by poison, entrap thee by some
treacherous device and never leave thee till he
hath ta'en thy life by some indirect means or
other;
for, I assure thee, and almost with tears I speak
it, there is not one so young and so villanous this
day living. I speak but brotherly of him; but
should I anatomize him to thee as he is, I must
blush and weep and thou must look pale and
wonder.

CHARLES
I am heartily glad I came hither to you. If he
come
to-morrow, I'll give him his payment: if ever he
go
alone again, I'll never wrestle for prize more:
and
so God keep your worship!

OLIVER
Farewell, good Charles.

Now will I stir this gamester: I hope I shall see
an end of him; for my soul, yet I know not why,
hates nothing more than he. Yet he's gentle,
never
schooled and yet learned, full of noble device, of
all sorts enchantingly beloved, and indeed so
much
in the heart of the world, and especially of my
own
people, who best know him, that I am altogether
misprised: but it shall not be so long; this
wrestler shall clear all: nothing remains but that
I kindle the boy thither; which now I'll go about.

*against me, his own brother. Do whatever you
think is best – in fact, I would be just as happy if
you broke his neck as his finger. You should be
careful, too, because if you do disgrace him, or
even if he does not beat you by a lot, he will
come against you with poison or he will trap
you by some dangerous plan, and he will never
leave until he has killed you, some way or
another.*
*I promise you, and it saddens me to tears to say
it, no man so young and yet so cruel and bad
exists except for him. And I am speaking as his
brother – if I were to talk to you as he really is, I
would blush and cry and you would look
shocked and amazed.*

*I am very glad I came here. If he fights me
tomorrow, then I will give him what he deserves.
If he can
walk without assistance after the fight, I will not
wrestle for money again.
God keep you well, your worship!*

Goodbye, Charles.

Exit CHARLES

*Now I will see what happens to this dandy
brother. I hope I see him killed, for honestly,
and I don't know why, I hate him more than
everything, even though he is nice, has never
been taught anything but is still educated, is
noble, is loved by all kinds of people, is loved in
fact by the whole world, and especially of my
people, who know him best. Because they love
him, they despise me – but it won't be this way
for long. The wrestler, Charles, will fix all of
this. All I have to do
is convince Orlando to fight tomorrow, which I
will do now.*

Exit

SCENE II. Lawn before the Duke's palace.

Enter CELIA and ROSALIND

CELIA
I pray thee, Rosalind, sweet my coz, be merry.

I hope that you are happy, Rosalind, my sweet cousin.

ROSALIND
Dear Celia, I show more mirth than I am mistress of;
and would you yet I were merrier? Unless you could
teach me to forget a banished father, you must not
learn me how to remember any extraordinary pleasure.

*Dear Celia, I present myself as happier than I really am,
and you want me to be even happier? Unless you can
teach me how to forget about my father and his banishment, you should not
expect me to remember such great pleasure.*

CELIA
Herein I see thou lovest me not with the full weight
that I love thee. If my uncle, thy banished father, had banished thy uncle, the duke my father, so thou
hadst been still with me, I could have taught my love to take thy father for mine: so wouldst thou, if the truth of thy love to me were so righteously tempered as mine is to thee.

*Now I see that you do not love me as fully as I love you. If my uncle, your banished father, had banished your uncle, my father the duke, and if
I was still here with you, then I would have been able to love your father as my own. You would be able to also, if your love for me was so strong and overpowering as mine is for you.*

ROSALIND
Well, I will forget the condition of my estate, to rejoice in yours.

Fine, then I will forget my own situation in order to be happy for you and rejoice in your situation.

CELIA
You know my father hath no child but I, nor none is
like to have: and, truly, when he dies, thou shalt be his heir, for what he hath taken away from thy
father perforce, I will render thee again in affection; by mine honour, I will; and when I break
that oath, let me turn monster: therefore, my sweet Rose, my dear Rose, be merry.

*You know my father has only me as his child, and is
not likely to have anymore. And, when he dies, you will
be his heir – what he took away from your father by force I will give to you in
love. I swear it by my own honor, and if I break that promise, than I hope I become a monster. Now, my
sweet, dear Rose, be happy.*

ROSALIND

From henceforth I will, coz, and devise sports. Let
me see; what think you of falling in love?

CELIA
Marry, I prithee, do, to make sport withal: but
love no man in good earnest; nor no further in sport
neither than with safety of a pure blush thou mayst
in honour come off again.

ROSALIND
What shall be our sport, then?

CELIA
Let us sit and mock the good housewife Fortune from
her wheel, that her gifts may henceforth be
bestowed equally.

ROSALIND
I would we could do so, for her benefits are
mightily misplaced, and the bountiful blind woman
doth most mistake in her gifts to women.

CELIA
'Tis true; for those that she makes fair she scarce
makes honest, and those that she makes honest she
makes very ill-favouredly.

ROSALIND
Nay, now thou goest from Fortune's office to
Nature's: Fortune reigns in gifts of the world,
not in the lineaments of Nature.

CELIA
No? when Nature hath made a fair creature, may she
not by Fortune fall into the fire? Though Nature
hath given us wit to flout at Fortune, hath not

From now on, I will be merry and come up with various games, for you, my cousin. Let's see: what do you think about falling in love.

Yes, please, let's do that and fall in love – but we should not love seriously, and we shouldn't play any game that we can't get out of safely, with a simple blush.

So what shall we do instead?

Let's sit here and make fun of Fortune, that loose housewife, and see if she will give her gifts more equally.

I wish we could get her to do that. Her gifts are so wrongly distributed, and that blind woman mistakes her gifts to women most of all.

It's true: whoever she makes beautiful, she rarely makes them faithful and pure, and those whom she makes pure, she also makes ugly.

No, you are not talking about Fortune now, you mean Nature: Fortune decides what we are given in the world, but Nature decides what we are given as humans.

Enter TOUCHSTONE

Really? When Nature makes a beautiful person, couldn't that person then fall into the fire because of Fortune, turning her ugly? And even though Nature endowed us with the intelligence

Fortune sent in this fool to cut off the argument?

to make fun of Fortune, didn't Fortune send this fool Touchstone to ruin our argument?

ROSALIND
Indeed, there is Fortune too hard for Nature, when
Fortune makes Nature's natural the cutter-off of Nature's wit.

Yes, and now Fortune is being difficult with Nature:
Fortune has made Nature's natural fool cut off two women whom Nature made naturally witty.

CELIA
Peradventure this is not Fortune's work neither, but
Nature's; who perceiveth our natural wits too dull
to reason of such goddesses and hath sent this natural for our whetstone; for always the dulness of
the fool is the whetstone of the wits. How now, wit! whither wander you?

Perhaps this is not Fortune's doing either, but is Nature's: Nature saw that we are not naturally smart enough
to talk about either goddess, and so sent us this natural fool to make us smarter. After all, the ignorance of
the fool always makes the wits of the smart person sharper. Hello, fool! Where are you off to?

TOUCHSTONE
Mistress, you must come away to your father.

Mistress, you must come see your father.

CELIA
Were you made the messenger?

And he sent you to take me away?

TOUCHSTONE
No, by mine honour, but I was bid to come for you.

By my honor, not to take you away like a police officer! But I was sent to get you.

ROSALIND
Where learned you that oath, fool?

Where did you learn an oath like that, "by my honor," you fool?

TOUCHSTONE
Of a certain knight that swore by his honour they
were good pancakes and swore by his honour the
mustard was naught: now I'll stand to it, the pancakes were naught and the mustard was good, and
yet was not the knight forsworn.

A knight I knew swore by his honor that the pancakes were good and he swore by his honor that the
mustard was not good – but truly, the pancakes were not good and the mustard was fine, and
yet still, since the knight had sworn, he had not lied.

CELIA
How prove you that, in the great heap of your knowledge?

How do you figure that? Prove it from your great amount of knowledge.

ROSALIND
Ay, marry, now unmuzzle your wisdom.

Yes, unleash all of your wisdom.

TOUCHSTONE
Stand you both forth now: stroke your chins,
and
swear by your beards that I am a knave.

*Then stand back, both of you. First stroke your chins and
swear by your beards that I am a rascal.*

CELIA
By our beards, if we had them, thou art.

By our beards (if we had them, that is), you are a rascal.

TOUCHSTONE
By my knavery, if I had it, then I were; but if you
swear by that that is not, you are not forsworn: no
more was this knight swearing by his honour, for he
never had any; or if he had, he had sworn it away
before ever he saw those pancakes or that mustard.

*And I swear by my trickery, if I had any, that I
am a rascal as well: but if you
swear by something that you don't have, then
even a lie doesn't break that oath.
The knight swore by his honor, but really he
never had any to begin with – or if he did, then
he lost it by making oaths
long before he saw the pancakes or the mustard.*

CELIA
Prithee, who is't that thou meanest?

Tell us, who are you talking about?

TOUCHSTONE
One that old Frederick, your father, loves.

A knight whom your father, old Frederick, loves.

CELIA
My father's love is enough to honour him: enough!
speak no more of him; you'll be whipped for taxation
one of these days.

*Then my father's love is enough to make him honorable! Now stop
and don't speak any more about him, or else you will be whipped for slander.
I'm sure you will some day anyway.*

TOUCHSTONE
The more pity, that fools may not speak wisely what
wise men do foolishly.

*It is sad that fools are not allowed to talk wisely about
the foolish actions of wise men.*

CELIA
By my troth, thou sayest true; for since the little
wit that fools have was silenced, the little foolery
that wise men have makes a great show. Here

*That's true: since the little
wisdom that fools might have has been silenced, the little foolishness
that wise men have ends up being obvious and*

comes
Monsieur Le Beau.

ROSALIND
With his mouth full of news.

CELIA
Which he will put on us, as pigeons feed their
young.

ROSALIND
Then shall we be news-crammed.

CELIA
All the better; we shall be the more marketable.

Bon jour, Monsieur Le Beau: what's the news?

LE BEAU
Fair princess, you have lost much good sport.

CELIA
Sport! of what colour?

LE BEAU
What colour, madam! how shall I answer you?

ROSALIND
As wit and fortune will.

TOUCHSTONE
Or as the Destinies decree.

CELIA
Well said: that was laid on with a trowel.

TOUCHSTONE
Nay, if I keep not my rank,--

ROSALIND
Thou losest thy old smell.

LE BEAU

*apparent. Here comes
Mister Le Beau.*

No doubt full of news to tell us.

*He will force it on us the same way that pigeons
feed their young.*

And then we shall be stuffed with news.

Good, a fatter bird is worth more anyway.

Enter LE BEAU

Hello, Mister Le Beau: what is new?

Fair princess, you are missing out on some fun.

Fun! What color of fun?

*What color, madam? I don't understand; how
am I supposed to respond to that?*

As your brain and luck allows you.

Or as the Fates say you will.

Well said: you laid that on thick.

If I don't keep my Jester's rank–

Then you'll lose your smell.

You amaze me, ladies: I would have told you of good
wrestling, which you have lost the sight of.

ROSALIND
You tell us the manner of the wrestling.

LE BEAU
I will tell you the beginning; and, if it please
your ladyships, you may see the end; for the best
is
yet to do; and here, where you are, they are
coming
to perform it.

CELIA
Well, the beginning, that is dead and buried.

LE BEAU
There comes an old man and his three sons,--

CELIA
I could match this beginning with an old tale.

LE BEAU
Three proper young men, of excellent growth
and presence.

ROSALIND
With bills on their necks, 'Be it known unto all
men
by these presents.'

LE BEAU
The eldest of the three wrestled with Charles,
the
duke's wrestler; which Charles in a moment
threw him
and broke three of his ribs, that there is little
hope of life in him: so he served the second, and
so the third. Yonder they lie; the poor old man,
their father, making such pitiful dole over them
that all the beholders take his part with weeping.

ROSALIND

*Ladies, you are confusing me. I wanted to tell
you of a good
wrestling match, which you have missed part of.*

Tell us more about this match.

*I will tell you about the beginning, and if you
find it interesting,
you can see the end, which is the best
part. In fact, they are coming here to finish the
match.*

*Well the beginning is over with, it's dead and
buried.*

An old man came with his three sons–

*This sounds like the beginning of an old folk
tale.*

*Three good and right young men, big and
strong, with a commanding presence.*

*With signs around their necks that say, "Let it
be known to everyone
by these presents.'*

*The oldest brother wrestled with Charles, the
duke's own wrestler, and Charles immediately
threw him and broke three of his ribs. It is
doubtful that he will survive. He did the same to
the second and to the third brother. They are
lying over there, and their poor old father
is crying so loudly and sadly over them
that everyone watching in the audience is
grieving as well.*

Alas!

Oh no!

TOUCHSTONE
But what is the sport, monsieur, that the ladies have lost?

So what is the fun part, sir, that you say the ladies have missed?

LE BEAU
Why, this that I speak of.

Why, what I just said.

TOUCHSTONE
Thus men may grow wiser every day: it is the first
time that ever I heard breaking of ribs was sport for ladies.

*Men must be getting smarter every day, since this is the first
time I have ever heard someone call broken ribs a fun sport for ladies to see.*

CELIA
Or I, I promise thee.

Me too, I promise.

ROSALIND
But is there any else longs to see this broken music
in his sides? is there yet another dotes upon rib-breaking? Shall we see this wrestling, cousin?

*But who else longs to hear the noise of breath pushed through broken ribs? And who but us would love to see
ribs being broken? Can we see the wrestling, cousin Celia?*

LE BEAU
You must, if you stay here; for here is the place appointed for the wrestling, and they are ready to
perform it.

You will if you stay here, since this is where they will finish the wrestling, and they are ready to keep going.

CELIA
Yonder, sure, they are coming: let us now stay and see it.

Yes – they are coming from over there. We should stay and watch.

Flourish. Enter DUKE FREDERICK, Lords, ORLANDO, CHARLES, and Attendants

LE BEAU

DUKE FREDERICK
Come on: since the youth will not be entreated, his
own peril on his forwardness.

*Come on, then. Since this young man won't listen to pleas to stop, he
risks his own life from his hardheadedness.*

ROSALIND
Is yonder the man?

Is that the man?

Even he, madam.

Yes it is, madam.

CELIA
Alas, he is too young! yet he looks successfully.

Oh, but he is too young! But he looks like he can handle himself well.

DUKE FREDERICK
How now, daughter and cousin! are you crept hither
to see the wrestling?

*Daughter and niece, what are you doing here? Have you come
to see the wrestling?*

ROSALIND
Ay, my liege, so please you give us leave.

Yes, my liege, and please allow us to watch.

DUKE FREDERICK
You will take little delight in it, I can tell you;
there is such odds in the man. In pity of the
challenger's youth I would fain dissuade him,
but he
will not be entreated. Speak to him, ladies; see if
you can move him.

*You will not enjoy it much, to be honest:
the odds are greatly against this young man.
Out of sadness for his youth, I have tried to
persuade him against fighting, but he
will not listen. Ladies, speak to him and see if
you can get him to give up.*

CELIA
Call him hither, good Monsieur Le Beau.

Call him to us, good Mister Le Beau.

DUKE FREDERICK
Do so: I'll not be by.

Yes, and I will leave you alone to talk.

LE BEAU
Monsieur the challenger, the princesses call for
you.

*Mister challenger, the princesses have called to
talk to you.*

ORLANDO
I attend them with all respect and duty.

I come to them with my respect and obedience.

ROSALIND
Young man, have you challenged Charles the
wrestler?

*Young man, have you really challenged Charles,
the duke's professional wrestler?*

ORLANDO
No, fair princess; he is the general challenger: I
come but in, as others do, to try with him the
strength of my youth.

*No, beautiful princess, he is the general
challenger. I, like many others, come up against
him to test my young strength.*

CELIA
Young gentleman, your spirits are too bold for
your

*Young man, you are too bold for your
age. You have already seen the awful effects of*

years. You have seen cruel proof of this man's strength: if you saw yourself with your eyes or knew yourself with your judgment, the fear of your
adventure would counsel you to a more equal enterprise. We pray you, for your own sake, to embrace your own safety and give over this attempt.

this wrestler's strength. You need to look at yourself, or know yourself honestly; then the proper fear of this plan will teach you to look for a less dangerous adventure. We beg you, for your sake, do the safe thing and give up this attempt to fight.

ROSALIND

Do, young sir; your reputation shall not therefore
be misprised: we will make it our suit to the duke
that the wrestling might not go forward.

Yes, do that, young sir. We will even make sure your reputation does not suffer by taking it upon ourselves to request the duke to cancel the wrestling match.

ORLANDO

I beseech you, punish me not with your hard thoughts; wherein I confess me much guilty, to deny
so fair and excellent ladies any thing. But let your fair eyes and gentle wishes go with me to my
trial: wherein if I be foiled, there is but one shamed that was never gracious; if killed, but one
dead that was willing to be so: I shall do my friends no wrong, for I have none to lament me, the
world no injury, for in it I have nothing; only in the world I fill up a place, which may be better supplied when I have made it empty.

Please do not punish me with your hard honesty. I confess that I would be very guilt to deny either of you beautiful ladies anything, but I would rather your beautiful eyes and good wishes follow me to the match. If I am beaten there, then only I get the shame, and I wasn't thought well of anyway. But if I am killed, then the one who dies was willing to die. I am not doing my friends anything wrong, since I do not have friends to cry for me, and I am not harming the world because I have nothing in the world — I only take up space, which might be better filled when I am out of it.

ROSALIND

The little strength that I have, I would it were with you.

I wish that the little strength I have goes with you.

CELIA

And mine, to eke out hers.

Mine as well, to join with hers.

ROSALIND

Fare you well: pray heaven I be deceived in you!

Good luck, and I pray that I am wrong about your chances!

CELIA

Your heart's desires be with you!

May whatever you desire be with you!

CHARLES
Come, where is this young gallant that is so desirous to lie with his mother earth?

Come on, where is that young playboy who wants to be buried and sleep with Mother Earth?

ORLANDO
Ready, sir; but his will hath in it a more modest working.

I am ready, sir – but I am aspiring to more modest things.

DUKE FREDERICK
You shall try but one fall.

You get only one round.

CHARLES
No, I warrant your grace, you shall not entreat him
to a second, that have so mightily persuaded him from a first.

I promise your grace, you won't have to beg him to fight in a second round, even though you couldn't keep him from a first round.

ORLANDO
You mean to mock me after, you should not have
mocked me before: but come your ways.

You should be mocking me after the fight, not before, but whatever you want.

ROSALIND
Now Hercules be thy speed, young man!

Be as fast as Hercules, young man!

CELIA
I would I were invisible, to catch the strong fellow by the leg.

I wish I was invisible so that I could grab onto Charles by the leg.

They wrestle

ROSALIND
O excellent young man!

What an excellent young man!

CELIA
If I had a thunderbolt in mine eye, I can tell who should down.

If I could shoot thunderbolts from my eyes, I can tell you who would be thrown down.

Shout. CHARLES is thrown

DUKE FREDERICK
No more, no more.

No more, stop.

ORLANDO
Yes, I beseech your grace: I am not yet well

Please, I beg you, your Grace, let us continue:

breathed.

I'm not yet out of breath.

DUKE FREDERICK
How dost thou, Charles?

And how are you doing, Charles?

LE BEAU
He cannot speak, my lord.

He can't speak, my lord.

DUKE FREDERICK
Bear him away. What is thy name, young man?

Carry him away. What is your name, young man?

ORLANDO
Orlando, my liege; the youngest son of Sir
Rowland de Boys.

Orlando, my liege, the youngest son of Sire Rowland de Boys.

DUKE FREDERICK
I would thou hadst been son to some man else:
The world esteem'd thy father honourable,
But I did find him still mine enemy:
Thou shouldst have better pleased me with this deed,
Hadst thou descended from another house.
But fare thee well; thou art a gallant youth:
I would thou hadst told me of another father.

I wish you had been someone else's son. The world held your father as very honorable, but I still considered him my enemy. Your victory would have please me more if you were from a different family. Still, I wish you well. You are a brave young man and I only wish you had told me you had another father.

Exeunt DUKE FREDERICK, train, and LE BEAU

CELIA
Were I my father, coz, would I do this?

Cousin, would I do this if I were my father?

ORLANDO
I am more proud to be Sir Rowland's son,
His youngest son; and would not change that calling,
To be adopted heir to Frederick.

I am proud to be Sir Rowland's youngest son, and would not change that even to become Frederick's adopted heir.

ROSALIND
My father loved Sir Rowland as his soul,
And all the world was of my father's mind:
Had I before known this young man his son,
I should have given him tears unto entreaties,
Ere he should thus have ventured.

My father loved Sir Rowland as much as his own soul, and everyone else shared his opinion. If I had known beforehand that he were his son, I would have begged him with tears not to go on with his plans.

CELIA
Gentle cousin,

Gentle cousin,

Let us go thank him and encourage him:
My father's rough and envious disposition
Sticks me at heart. Sir, you have well deserved:
If you do keep your promises in love
But justly, as you have exceeded all promise,
Your mistress shall be happy.

*my father's jealous meanness
upsets me. Sir, you did very well in the match,
and if you are able to love
like that, even better than how others think you
can, then your wife will be very happy.*

Giving him a chain from her neck

ROSALIND
Gentleman,

Gentleman,

Wear this for me, one out of suits with fortune,
That could give more, but that her hand lacks
means.
Shall we go, coz?

*Where this necklace for me, someone who has
been unlucky and thus cannot give you anything
greater. Shall we leave, cousin?*

CELIA
Ay. Fare you well, fair gentleman.

Yes. Best of luck to you, fair gentleman.

ORLANDO
Can I not say, I thank you? My better parts
Are all thrown down, and that which here stands
up
Is but a quintain, a mere lifeless block.

*I can't even say thank you? Really? All of my
best parts, like my ability to speak, are back on
the wrestling mat. The only thing left, which
stands here is a dummy, a lifeless stone.*

ROSALIND
He calls us back: my pride fell with my
fortunes;
I'll ask him what he would. Did you call, sir?
Sir, you have wrestled well and overthrown
More than your enemies.

*He is calling towards us to come back. My luck
fell, and like it my pride did too.
I'll ask him what he wanted. Did you call to us,
sir? Sir, you have fought well, and you have
conquered more than your enemies.*

CELIA
Will you go, coz?

Can we go now, cousin?

ROSALIND
Have with you. Fare you well.

Fine, fine. Good luck, sir.

Exeunt ROSALIND and CELIA

ORLANDO
What passion hangs these weights upon my
tongue?
I cannot speak to her, yet she urged conference.
O poor Orlando, thou art overthrown!
Or Charles or something weaker masters thee.

*What are these passionate feelings that are
blocking my tongue?
I can't seem to say anything to her, and she even
sought to talk to me.
O poor me! I have been conquered!
Either Charles or else something weaker and
prettier has overcome me.*

LE BEAU

Good sir, I do in friendship counsel you
To leave this place. Albeit you have deserved
High commendation, true applause and love,
Yet such is now the duke's condition
That he misconstrues all that you have done.
The duke is humorous; what he is indeed,
More suits you to conceive than I to speak of.

ORLANDO

I thank you, sir: and, pray you, tell me this:
Which of the two was daughter of the duke
That here was at the wrestling?

LE BEAU

Neither his daughter, if we judge by manners;
But yet indeed the lesser is his daughter
The other is daughter to the banish'd duke,
And here detain'd by her usurping uncle,
To keep his daughter company; whose loves
Are dearer than the natural bond of sisters.
But I can tell you that of late this duke
Hath ta'en displeasure 'gainst his gentle niece,
Grounded upon no other argument
But that the people praise her for her virtues
And pity her for her good father's sake;
And, on my life, his malice 'gainst the lady
Will suddenly break forth. Sir, fare you well:
Hereafter, in a better world than this,
I shall desire more love and knowledge of you.

ORLANDO

I rest much bounden to you: fare you well.

Thus must I from the smoke into the smother;
From tyrant duke unto a tyrant brother:
But heavenly Rosalind!

Re-enter LE BEAU

*Sir, in friendship I advise you
to leave this place. While it is true that you have
deserved high praise, applause, and love,
the duke is now of a strange mood and he
misconstrues your actions. He is very moody,
and I'm sure you can imagine what I mean
without me putting words to it.*

*Thank you sir, and please, tell me:
which girl is the duke's daughter
of the two who were at the match?*

*If you are judging by their manners, neither –
but in fact the smaller one is the duke's
daughter, and the other is the daughter of the
banished duke, kept here by her uncle after
usurping the throne to keep his daughter
company. Their love is stronger than the natural
bond of sisters. But lately, the duke
has become displeased with his niece
for no other reason than the fact that she is
praised by everyone for her virtues,
and pitied for the sake of her good father.
I swear on my life, his ill will towards her
will become manifest soon. Sir, best of luck to
you. Some time later, in a better world than this
one, I would like to get to know you better.*

I owe you much, Goodbye.

Exit LE BEAU

*So I must go from the smoke to the fire –
from the tyrant duke to his tyrant brother.
But heavenly Rosalind!*

Exit

SCENE III. A room in the palace.

Enter CELIA and ROSALIND

CELIA
Why, cousin! why, Rosalind! Cupid have
mercy! not a word?

*Dear cousin! Dear Rosalind! Cupid have mercy!
You won't say a single word??*

ROSALIND
Not one to throw at a dog.

I don't even have one to throw to a dog.

CELIA
No, thy words are too precious to be cast away
upon
curs; throw some of them at me; come, lame me
with reasons.

*Your words are worth too much to be thrown
away at dogs. Throw some at me instead. Hit me
with your reasoning like you would hit a dog
with stones.*

ROSALIND
Then there were two cousins laid up; when the
one
should be lamed with reasons and the other mad
without any.

*If I did that, then the two of us would be sick and
injured: one
made lame from being hit with reasons, and the
other made crazy from no reason.*

CELIA
But is all this for your father?

Is this about your father?

ROSALIND
No, some of it is for my child's father. O, how
full of briers is this working-day world!

*No, but some is for my future child's father.
How injurious and thorny is this working-day,
wearisome world!*

CELIA
They are but burs, cousin, thrown upon thee in
holiday foolery: if we walk not in the trodden
paths our very petticoats will catch them.

*The thorns are just burrs, cousin, that you have
caught from taking a foolish holiday from the
right path: if you don't walk on the
paths that are already well-trodden, then of
course they will attach to our petticoats.*

ROSALIND
I could shake them off my coat: these burs are in
my heart.

*I could shake them off of my coat – but these
burrs are in my heart.*

CELIA
Hem them away.

Cough them up.

ROSALIND
I would try, if I could cry 'hem' and have him.

I would try, as long as crying "hem" would

CELIA
Come, come, wrestle with thy affections.

ROSALIND
O, they take the part of a better wrestler than
myself!

CELIA
O, a good wish upon you! you will try in time,
in
despite of a fall. But, turning these jests out of
service, let us talk in good earnest: is it
possible, on such a sudden, you should fall into
so
strong a liking with old Sir Rowland's youngest
son?

ROSALIND
The duke my father loved his father dearly.

CELIA
Doth it therefore ensue that you should love his
son
dearly? By this kind of chase, I should hate him,
for my father hated his father dearly; yet I hate
not Orlando.

ROSALIND
No, faith, hate him not, for my sake.

CELIA
Why should I not? doth he not deserve well?

ROSALIND
Let me love him for that, and do you love him
because I do. Look, here comes the duke.

CELIA
With his eyes full of anger.

DUKE FREDERICK
Mistress, dispatch you with your safest haste
And get you from our court.

---

allow me to have him.

Come on, now. Fight against your feelings.

*But they are for such a better fighter than
myself!*

*That's a good wish then! You will fight him in
time
and then falling to him will be good. But let's
not only joke
about this. Let's talk sincerely: is it
possible that you so quickly have fallen
in love with old Sir Rowland's youngest son?*

My father, the old duke, loved his father a lot.

*Does it follow that you would thus love his son
a lot? By this logic, I should hate him,
since my father hated his father a lot. Yet, I
don't hate
Orlando.*

No, please, do not hate him, for my sake.

Why shouldn't I? Doesn't he deserve it?

*Let me love him, because he deserves that, and
then you can love him
because I do. Look, here comes the Duke.*

And his eyes look angry.

Enter DUKE FREDERICK, with Lords

*Mistress, get your things together as quickly as
possible and leave my court.*

ROSALIND
Me, uncle?

Me, uncle?

DUKE FREDERICK
You, cousin
Within these ten days if that thou be'st found
So near our public court as twenty miles,
Thou diest for it.

You, niece.
If in ten days you are found
within twenty miles of my court,
you will die as punishment.

ROSALIND
I do beseech your grace,
Let me the knowledge of my fault bear with me:
If with myself I hold intelligence
Or have acquaintance with mine own desires,
If that I do not dream or be not frantic,--
As I do trust I am not--then, dear uncle,
Never so much as in a thought unborn
Did I offend your highness.

I beg you, my grace,
Tell me what faults you have with me.
If I know myself
and my own desires well,
and as long as I am not dreaming or crazy –
which I don't think I am – then, dear uncle,
I cannot find even a thought
that was against your highness.

DUKE FREDERICK
Thus do all traitors:
If their purgation did consist in words,
They are as innocent as grace itself:
Let it suffice thee that I trust thee not.

Spoken like a true traitor.
If a traitor's salvation was due to words only,
then they would all be as innocent as divine
grace itself. Just be certain: I don't trust you.

ROSALIND
Yet your mistrust cannot make me a traitor:
Tell me whereon the likelihood depends.

But you can't call me a traitor only from
mistrust:
please tell me what your suspicion comes from.

DUKE FREDERICK
Thou art thy father's daughter; there's enough.

You are your father's daughter – that's enough
for me.

ROSALIND
So was I when your highness took his dukedom;
So was I when your highness banish'd him:
Treason is not inherited, my lord;
Or, if we did derive it from our friends,
What's that to me? my father was no traitor:
Then, good my liege, mistake me not so much
To think my poverty is treacherous.

I was his daughter when your highness took
over his position, and I was also when your
highness banished. My lord, treason is not
inherited, but even if it is and can come from
our friends or family, what would that matter?
My father wasn't a traitor. Good duke, do not
make the mistake that because my father is
gone, I have become treacherous.

CELIA
Dear sovereign, hear me speak.

Dear duke, let me say something.

DUKE FREDERICK

Ay, Celia; we stay'd her for your sake,
Else had she with her father ranged along.

CELIA
I did not then entreat to have her stay;
It was your pleasure and your own remorse:
I was too young that time to value her;
But now I know her: if she be a traitor,
Why so am I; we still have slept together,
Rose at an instant, learn'd, play'd, eat together,
And wheresoever we went, like Juno's swans,
Still we went coupled and inseparable.

DUKE FREDERICK
She is too subtle for thee; and her smoothness,
Her very silence and her patience
Speak to the people, and they pity her.
Thou art a fool: she robs thee of thy name;
And thou wilt show more bright and seem more virtuous
When she is gone. Then open not thy lips:
Firm and irrevocable is my doom
Which I have pass'd upon her; she is banish'd.

CELIA
Pronounce that sentence then on me, my liege:
I cannot live out of her company.

DUKE FREDERICK
You are a fool. You, niece, provide yourself:
If you outstay the time, upon mine honour,
And in the greatness of my word, you die.

O my poor Rosalind, whither wilt thou go?
Wilt thou change fathers? I will give thee mine.
I charge thee, be not thou more grieved than I am.

ROSALIND
I have more cause.

CELIA

Yes, Celia. We kept her here for you.
Otherwise she would have gone with her father.

I did not beg you to make her stay.
No, you wanted to, and you felt bad about
separating us. I was too young then to truly
value her, but know I know her well, and if she
is a traitor, than so am I. After all, we have slept
together, gotten up together, learned and played
and ate together.
Wherever we went we were like Juno's swans,
together as a couple, and inseparable.

She is too clever and tricky for you. Her
smoothness, her patience, and her very silence
all speak to the people and maker them pity her.
You are a fool and she is ruining your name –
after all, you will look brighter and more
virtuous
when she is gone. Don't say anything else.
The fate that I have decided for her
is firm and unchangeable: she is banished.

Then banish me as well, my liege:
I can't live without her.

You are a fool. Niece, prepare yourself.
I swear by my honor and my word, if you stay
longer than I allow,
you will die.

Exeunt DUKE FREDERICK and Lords CELIA

My poor Rosalind, where will you go?
Can you change fathers? You can have mine.
Please, do not be sadder than me.

But I have more reason to be.

Thou hast not, cousin;
Prithee be cheerful: know'st thou not, the duke
Hath banish'd me, his daughter?

ROSALIND
That he hath not.

CELIA
No, hath not? Rosalind lacks then the love
Which teacheth thee that thou and I am one:
Shall we be sunder'd? shall we part, sweet girl?
No: let my father seek another heir.
Therefore devise with me how we may fly,
Whither to go and what to bear with us;
And do not seek to take your change upon you,
To bear your griefs yourself and leave me out;
For, by this heaven, now at our sorrows pale,
Say what thou canst, I'll go along with thee.

ROSALIND
Why, whither shall we go?

CELIA
To seek my uncle in the forest of Arden.

ROSALIND
Alas, what danger will it be to us,
Maids as we are, to travel forth so far!
Beauty provoketh thieves sooner than gold.

CELIA
I'll put myself in poor and mean attire
And with a kind of umber smirch my face;
The like do you: so shall we pass along
And never stir assailants.

ROSALIND
Were it not better,
Because that I am more than common tall,
That I did suit me all points like a man?
A gallant curtle-axe upon my thigh,
A boar-spear in my hand; and--in my heart
Lie there what hidden woman's fear there will--
We'll have a swashing and a martial outside,
As many other mannish cowards have
That do outface it with their semblances.

No you don't, cousin.
Please, be cheerful. Don't you know that the
duke has banished me, his own daughter, also?

No, he hasn't.

He hasn't? Then you still do not know about the
love that says that you and I are one:
Can we be split? Can we be parted?
No. My father can seek another heir.
Therefore let's plan how we should leave,
where we should go, and what we should bring
with us. Don't try to take this change of fortune
on yourself, to bear your sadness alone and
leave me out of it. I swear by heaven that, even
now, as our sorrows make us pale,
no matter what you say, I will go with you.

Where would we go?

To find my uncle in the forest of Arden.

Oh, it is so dangerous for us,
single, pretty women, to travel so far alone!
Our beauty will provoke thieves to steal much
quicker than gold will.

Then I will dress myself in ugly clothing
And smudge my face with a dark brown color.
You do the same, and then we will be able to
pass without possible muggers noticing us.

Wouldn't it be better
if, because I am taller than average,
I dressed up like a man?
I can put a sword at my hip, and a large spear
in my hand. Then – even if in my heart there is
still the natural fear a woman has – we will look
warlike and will walk like a swagger, like manly
cowards do who look outwardly differently than
they feel inwardly.

CELIA

What shall I call thee when thou art a man?

What should I call you when you are a man?

ROSALIND

I'll have no worse a name than Jove's own page;
And therefore look you call me Ganymede.
But what will you be call'd?

*I will have a name just as good as Jove's
messenger, so you should call me Ganymede.
What will I call you?*

CELIA

Something that hath a reference to my state.
No longer Celia, but Aliena.

*Something that refers to my state, become a
stranger from home:
don't call me Celia, but Aliena.*

ROSALIND

But, cousin, what if we assay'd to steal
The clownish fool out of your father's court?
Would he not be a comfort to our travel?

*Cousin, what if we tried to take
the jester away from your father's court?
Wouldn't he be a comfort for us while we
travel?*

CELIA

He'll go along o'er the wide world with me;
Leave me alone to woo him. Let's away,
And get our jewels and our wealth together,
Devise the fittest time and safest way
To hide us from pursuit that will be made
After my flight. Now go we in content
To liberty and not to banishment.

*He will go all over the world with me if I ask –
I will handle wooing him. Let's go
and get out jewels and money together
and plan the best time and best path
to keep us from being pursued after
I run away from the court. Now we can go
happily
towards our freedom, and not in banishment.*

Exeunt

Act II

SCENE I. The Forest of Arden.

DUKE SENIOR

Now, my co-mates and brothers in exile,
Hath not old custom made this life more sweet
Than that of painted pomp? Are not these woods
More free from peril than the envious court?
Here feel we but the penalty of Adam,
The seasons' difference, as the icy fang
And churlish chiding of the winter's wind,
Which, when it bites and blows upon my body,
Even till I shrink with cold, I smile and say
'This is no flattery: these are counsellors
That feelingly persuade me what I am.'
Sweet are the uses of adversity,
Which, like the toad, ugly and venomous,
Wears yet a precious jewel in his head;
And this our life exempt from public haunt
Finds tongues in trees, books in the running brooks,
Sermons in stones and good in every thing.
I would not change it.

AMIENS

Happy is your grace,
That can translate the stubbornness of fortune
Into so quiet and so sweet a style.

DUKE SENIOR

Come, shall we go and kill us venison?
And yet it irks me the poor dappled fools,
Being native burghers of this desert city,
Should in their own confines with forked heads
Have their round haunches gored.

First Lord

Indeed, my lord,
The melancholy Jaques grieves at that,
And, in that kind, swears you do more usurp
Than doth your brother that hath banish'd you.
To-day my Lord of Amiens and myself
Did steal behind him as he lay along

---

*Now, my friends and brothers in exile with me,
hasn't the comparison with our old life made
this one even better than that in the royal
courts? Aren't these woods safer and freer than
life was there, where everyone was jealous?
Here, we only face the consequences from
Adam's sin: the changing seasons, the coldness
and the icy cruelty of winter's wind. The wind
blows and bites our bodies until we hunch over
to protect against the cold, but even then, I must
smile and think, "This is much different than the
flattery of the courts: this wind is an advisor
that tells me exactly who I am." Adversity and
hardship can have positives, like an ugly,
venomous toad who is still fabled to have a
jewel in his head. Our life here is free from the
public needs and instead we can listen to trees,
read the streams, listen to sermons from stones,
and find the good in everything. I would not
change our situation.*

*You grace is blessed
that you can turn such bad fortune
into such a quiet and sweet lifestyle.*

*Should we go and hunt some deer?
Still, it does upset me that those poor spotted
fools who are the native citizens of this deserted
city should in their own homes
be gored with arrows in their sides.*

*Yes, my lord,
and sad Jacques cries over it.
He even swears that you do more usurping here
than your brother did when he banished you.
Today, the Lord of Amiens and myself
quietly came up behind him as he was laying*

Under an oak whose antique root peeps out
Upon the brook that brawls along this wood:
To the which place a poor sequester'd stag,
That from the hunter's aim had ta'en a hurt,
Did come to languish, and indeed, my lord,
The wretched animal heaved forth such groans
That their discharge did stretch his leathern coat
Almost to bursting, and the big round tears
Coursed one another down his innocent nose
In piteous chase; and thus the hairy fool
Much marked of the melancholy Jaques,
Stood on the extremest verge of the swift brook,
Augmenting it with tears.

DUKE SENIOR
But what said Jaques?
Did he not moralize this spectacle?

First Lord
O, yes, into a thousand similes.
First, for his weeping into the needless stream;
'Poor deer,' quoth he, 'thou makest a testament
As worldlings do, giving thy sum of more
To that which had too much:' then, being there alone,
Left and abandon'd of his velvet friends,
"Tis right:' quoth he; 'thus misery doth part
The flux of company:' anon a careless herd,
Full of the pasture, jumps along by him
And never stays to greet him; 'Ay' quoth Jaques,
'Sweep on, you fat and greasy citizens;
'Tis just the fashion: wherefore do you look
Upon that poor and broken bankrupt there?'
Thus most invectively he pierceth through
The body of the country, city, court,
Yea, and of this our life, swearing that we
Are mere usurpers, tyrants and what's worse,
To fright the animals and to kill them up
In their assign'd and native dwelling-place.

DUKE SENIOR
And did you leave him in this contemplation?

Second Lord
We did, my lord, weeping and commenting

beneath an oak tree whose old root sticks out of
the ground near a stream that runs along the
forest. There, a poor, cornered stag,
hurt from a hunter's bow and arrow,
had come to lay in pain – truly, my lord,
the damned animal groaned so loudly and
heavily that when it groaned, it stretched its
body almost until it burst. Big round tears
fell down his innocent nose,
chasing after each other, as the hairy beast,
watched closely by sad Jacques,
stood close the edge of the stream
and filled it with its own tears.

But did Jacques said anything?
He must have made a moral of the scene.

O yes, and he compared it to a thousand other
things. First he talked about the deer weeping
into the stream and said, "Poor deer, you testify
just like a human, giving more
to that which already has too much." Then, on
the deer being alone
and abandoned by his velvet furred friends,
said, "It is right for a miserable creature
to leave the company of its friends."
Immediately then a careless herd,
filled with pasture grass, jumped by him
but did not stop at all, and Jacques said, "Yes,
run on, you fat and ugly citizens:
that's exactly what happens – why would you
stop and look at this poor and broken one
here?" In this way he angrily pierced
the body of the country, city, court,
and even our very lives by swearing that we
are usurpers and tryants
that frighten the animals and seek to kill them
in their own, native homes.

Did you leave him as he was thinking this?

We did, my lord. We left as he was weeping and

Upon the sobbing deer.

talking about the also-crying deer.

DUKE SENIOR
Show me the place:
I love to cope him in these sullen fits,
For then he's full of matter.

Show me where he is.
I love to talk with him when he is sad like this
because he is full of things to say.

First Lord
I'll bring you to him straight.

I'll bring you right to him.

Exeunt

SCENE II. A room in the palace.

`Enter DUKE FREDERICK, with Lords

DUKE FREDERICK
Can it be possible that no man saw them?
It cannot be: some villains of my court
Are of consent and sufferance in this.

Is it possible that no one saw them?
That can't be: some scoundrels in the court
must have consented to their plan and let it
happen.

First Lord
I cannot hear of any that did see her.
The ladies, her attendants of her chamber,
Saw her abed, and in the morning early
They found the bed untreasured of their
mistress.

I haven't heard of anyone who saw her.
Her bedroom attendants
saw her go to bed, and early this morning
they found the bed empty, without their mistress
in it.

Second Lord
My lord, the roynish clown, at whom so oft
Your grace was wont to laugh, is also missing.
Hisperia, the princess' gentlewoman,
Confesses that she secretly o'erheard
Your daughter and her cousin much commend
The parts and graces of the wrestler
That did but lately foil the sinewy Charles;
And she believes, wherever they are gone,
That youth is surely in their company.

My lord, that mangy clown, whom so often
you laughed at, is also gone.
Hisperia, the princess' gentlewoman,
has confessed that she secretly overheard
your daughter and her cousin praise
the appearance and the movements of the
wrestler who recently overthrew the strong
Charles. She believes that wherever they have
gone, the young wrestler is in their company.

DUKE FREDERICK
Send to his brother; fetch that gallant hither;
If he be absent, bring his brother to me;
I'll make him find him: do this suddenly,
And let not search and inquisition quail
To bring again these foolish runaways.

Send someone to his brother and fetch that
dandy Orlando here –
and if he is gone, bring Oliver to me.
I'll make him find Orlando. Do this quickly,
and do not stop searching and investigating
until you bring back these foolish runaways.

Exeunt

SCENE III. Before OLIVER'S house.

Enter ORLANDO and ADAM, meeting

ORLANDO

Who's there?

Who's there?

ADAM

What, my young master? O, my gentle master!
O my sweet master! O you memory
Of old Sir Rowland! why, what make you here?
Why are you virtuous? why do people love you?
And wherefore are you gentle, strong and
valiant?
Why would you be so fond to overcome
The bonny priser of the humorous duke?
Your praise is come too swiftly home before
you.
Know you not, master, to some kind of men
Their graces serve them but as enemies?
No more do yours: your virtues, gentle master,
Are sanctified and holy traitors to you.
O, what a world is this, when what is comely
Envenoms him that bears it!

My young, gentle master!
O my sweet master! You memory
of old Sir Rowland! What are you doing here?
Why are you so good and kind? Why do people
love you? Why are you so gentle, strong, and
brave? Why was it your desire to fight and
overthrow the fighter of the moody duke?
Your praise has come back against you.
Don't you know, master, that for some men,
their graceful qualities become their own
enemies? The same thing happens with yours:
your virtues, gentle master, are, even though
they are pure and holy, also traitors to you.
O what a world this is when the qualities that
are pleasant and good
poison the one who has those qualities!

ORLANDO

Why, what's the matter?

What is the matter?

ADAM

O unhappy youth!
Come not within these doors; within this roof
The enemy of all your graces lives:
Your brother--no, no brother; yet the son--
Yet not the son, I will not call him son
Of him I was about to call his father--
Hath heard your praises, and this night he means
To burn the lodging where you use to lie
And you within it: if he fail of that,
He will have other means to cut you off.
I overheard him and his practises.
This is no place; this house is but a butchery:
Abhor it, fear it, do not enter it.

O unhappy youth!
Do not walk through these doors. Under this
roof lives the enemy of your goodness:
your brother, Oliver. —No, not your brother, but
your father's son – no, not son either. I will not
call him son if that implies he is the son of your
father. Oliver has heard about the praises for
you, and tonight he intends to burn the house
where you use to sleep with you in it. And if that
were to fail, he would have other ways to kill
you. I overheard him and his plans.
This is no place for you. This house is a
butchery: hate it, fear it, and do not go into it.

ORLANDO

Why, whither, Adam, wouldst thou have me go?

ADAM
No matter whither, so you come not here.

It doesn't matter where, just do not come here.

ORLANDO
What, wouldst thou have me go and beg my
food?
Or with a base and boisterous sword enforce
A thievish living on the common road?
This I must do, or know not what to do:
Yet this I will not do, do how I can;
I rather will subject me to the malice
Of a diverted blood and bloody brother.

Would you want me to go and beg for food?
Or take a well-used sword in order to make
a thief's living by the side of the road?
This is all that is left for me to do, or else
something I don't know –
yet this I won't do, even if I could.
I would rather subject myself to the evil
of an estranged and bloodthirsty brother.

ADAM
But do not so. I have five hundred crowns,
The thrifty hire I saved under your father,
Which I did store to be my foster-nurse
When service should in my old limbs lie lame
And unregarded age in corners thrown:
Take that, and He that doth the ravens feed,
Yea, providently caters for the sparrow,
Be comfort to my age! Here is the gold;
And all this I give you. Let me be your servant:
Though I look old, yet I am strong and lusty;
For in my youth I never did apply
Hot and rebellious liquors in my blood,
Nor did not with unbashful forehead woo
The means of weakness and debility;
Therefore my age is as a lusty winter,
Frosty, but kindly: let me go with you;
I'll do the service of a younger man
In all your business and necessities.

Do not do that. I have five hundred crowns,
all saved while working under your father
and stored for my retirement
when I am too old and lame to give service to
anyone, when I am so old that I am thrown in a
corner and forgotten. Take that with you, and
God who feeds the ravens and cares for the
sparrow will watch over me in my age! Here is
my money, and all of it I give to you. Let me be
your servant still: though I look old, I am still
strong and energetic.
In my youth, I never drank evil liquors
nor did I recklessly test
my means and abilities:
therefore my age is like windy winter:
frosty, but kind. Let me go with you
and I will help you as if I were a younger man
in all of your business and needs.

ORLANDO
O good old man, how well in thee appears
The constant service of the antique world,
When service sweat for duty, not for meed!
Thou art not for the fashion of these times,
Where none will sweat but for promotion,
And having that, do choke their service up
Even with the having: it is not so with thee.
But, poor old man, thou prunest a rotten tree,
That cannot so much as a blossom yield
In lieu of all thy pains and husbandry
But where, Adam, would you have me go?

O good old man, in you I see
the constant service that used to be common in
the old world, when one served out of duty, not
just for money You are not built for these times
where no one will work hard except for
promotion, and when they get that, stop their
work almost immediately. That's not how you
are. But, poor old man, by coming me you are
trimming a rotten tree that cannot yield even a
single blossom, even with all of the pain and
But come thy ways; well go along together,

And ere we have thy youthful wages spent,
We'll light upon some settled low content.

ADAM
Master, go on, and I will follow thee,
To the last gasp, with truth and loyalty.
From seventeen years till now almost fourscore
Here lived I, but now live here no more.
At seventeen years many their fortunes seek;
But at fourscore it is too late a week:
Yet fortune cannot recompense me better
Than to die well and not my master's debtor.

care you give to it. But come anyway, we will go along together and before we have spent your money, we will find some way to make a happy living.

Master, go forward and I will follow you until my last breath with loyalty and faithfulness. From when I was seventeen years old until now, almost sixty, I have lived here, and now I will live here no longer. At seventeen, many men leave to look for their fortunes, for wealth – at sixty it is too late for that. Yet, there is no greater fortune for me now than to die without owing my master anything.

Exeunt

SCENE IV. The Forest of Arden.

Enter ROSALIND for Ganymede, CELIA for Aliena, and TOUCHSTONE

ROSALIND
O Jupiter, how weary are my spirits!

O Jupiter, my spirits are so tired!

TOUCHSTONE
I care not for my spirits, if my legs were not weary.

I wouldn't really care about my spirits if my legs weren't so tired.

ROSALIND
I could find in my heart to disgrace my man's apparel and to cry like a woman; but I must comfort
the weaker vessel, as doublet and hose ought to show
itself courageous to petticoat: therefore courage, good Aliena!

*I would cry out from my heart against wearing a man's clothing, like a woman would, but I must instead comfort
the weaker sex, just as anyone wearing men's clothing must be
brave and courageous to one wearing a dress. Therefore, be strong,
good Aliena!*

CELIA
I pray you, bear with me; I cannot go no further.

Please, bear with me: I can't go any further.

TOUCHSTONE
For my part, I had rather bear with you than bear you; yet I should bear no cross if I did bear you, for I think you have no money in your purse.

*As for me, I would rather bear with you than bear you and carry you. Yet, it would not be like bearing a cross to carry you
since I don't think that you have any money with crosses on them with you.*

ROSALIND
Well, this is the forest of Arden.

This is the forest of Arden.

TOUCHSTONE
Ay, now am I in Arden; the more fool I; when I was
at home, I was in a better place: but travellers must be content.

*Yes, and now I am a bigger fool for being in Arden. When I was
at home, I was in a better place – but a traveller should be happy regardless.*

ROSALIND
Ay, be so, good Touchstone.

Yes, be happy, good Touchstone.

Enter CORIN and SILVIUS

Look you, who comes here; a young man and an old in

Look, here comes a young man and an old man in a

solemn talk.

serious discussion.

CORIN
That is the way to make her scorn you still.

But doing that is how you will make her continue to dislike you.

SILVIUS
O Corin, that thou knew'st how I do love her!

O Corin, if only you knew how much I love her!

CORIN
I partly guess; for I have loved ere now.

I can guess, since I used to be in love once.

SILVIUS
No, Corin, being old, thou canst not guess,
Though in thy youth thou wast as true a lover
As ever sigh'd upon a midnight pillow:
But if thy love were ever like to mine--
As sure I think did never man love so--
How many actions most ridiculous
Hast thou been drawn to by thy fantasy?

No, Corin, you are old and so you can't really guess. If in your youth you were as in love as a lover who cries into his pillow late at night, and if your love was ever as strong as mine – which I think no love ever was – then how many ridiculous actions did you do out of your fantasies?

CORIN
Into a thousand that I have forgotten.

Thousands that I have forgotten.

SILVIUS
O, thou didst then ne'er love so heartily!
If thou remember'st not the slightest folly
That ever love did make thee run into,
Thou hast not loved:
Or if thou hast not sat as I do now,
Wearying thy hearer in thy mistress' praise,
Thou hast not loved:
Or if thou hast not broke from company
Abruptly, as my passion now makes me,
Thou hast not loved.
O Phebe, Phebe, Phebe!

Then you never loved as strong as I do! If you do not remember the slightest foolish action that you ever did because of your love, than you have not truly loved. Or, if you have not sat like this, tiring your listener with praise for your mistress, than you have not truly loved. Or if you have not left the company of others abruptly, as my feelings made me do, than you have not truly loved. O Phebe, Phebe, Phebe!

Exit

ROSALIND
Alas, poor shepherd! searching of thy wound,
I have by hard adventure found mine own.

O, poor shepherd! What you have said about your heartache reminds me of my own.

TOUCHSTONE
And I mine. I remember, when I was in love I broke
my sword upon a stone and bid him take that for

It reminds me of mine, too. I remember when I was in love, and I broke my sword on a stone and told it, "Take that!"

coming a-night to Jane Smile; and I remember the

kissing of her batlet and the cow's dugs that her pretty chopt hands had milked; and I remember the

wooing of a peascod instead of her, from whom I took

two cods and, giving her them again, said with weeping tears 'Wear these for my sake.' We that are

true lovers run into strange capers; but as all is mortal in nature, so is all nature in love mortal in folly.

ROSALIND
Thou speakest wiser than thou art ware of.

TOUCHSTONE
Nay, I shall ne'er be ware of mine own wit till I break my shins against it.

ROSALIND
Jove, Jove! this shepherd's passion
Is much upon my fashion.

TOUCHSTONE
And mine; but it grows something stale with me.

CELIA
I pray you, one of you question yond man
If he for gold will give us any food:
I faint almost to death.

TOUCHSTONE
Holla, you clown!

ROSALIND
Peace, fool: he's not thy kinsman.

CORIN
Who calls?

TOUCHSTONE
Your betters, sir.

CORIN

for seeing my love, Jane Smile, at night. I also kissed both her laundry washing stick and the cow udders, which
she touched with her pretty hands. And I remember
wooing a pea plant in her name, and then taking two pea pods and giving them to her, begging while crying, "Wear these for my sake." We who are
true lovers will do strange things – but everything
is mortal, even the foolishness of love.

You are saying wiser things than you know.

I'll never know my own wit until I break my shins against it.

Oh, God! This shepherd's love is very much like my own state.

And mine – but I am beginning to get over it.

Please, one of you ask that man if he will sell us any food:
I feel like I will faint.

Hello! You clown!

Be quiet, you fool: he is not related to you.

Who is calling?

Those better than you, sir.

Else are they very wretched.

If they weren't, they would be very wretched.

ROSALIND
Peace, I say. Good even to you, friend.

Be quiet, Touchstone. Good evening, friend.

CORIN
And to you, gentle sir, and to you all.

And to you, gentle sir, and all of you.

ROSALIND
I prithee, shepherd, if that love or gold
Can in this desert place buy entertainment,
Bring us where we may rest ourselves and feed:
Here's a young maid with travel much oppress'd
And faints for succor.

Please, shepherd, I would like to know if love or money can in this foreign and deserted place get us anything here. If so, take us to where we can rest and find food – this young lady is tired from a lot of traveling and is faint with hunger.

CORIN
Fair sir, I pity her
And wish, for her sake more than for mine own,
My fortunes were more able to relieve her;
But I am shepherd to another man
And do not shear the fleeces that I graze:
My master is of churlish disposition
And little recks to find the way to heaven
By doing deeds of hospitality:
Besides, his cote, his flocks and bounds of feed
Are now on sale, and at our sheepcote now,
By reason of his absence, there is nothing
That you will feed on; but what is, come see.
And in my voice most welcome shall you be.

*Good sir, I pity her
and wish for her sake, not for my own benefit, that I was fortunate enough to be able to help her. But I am a shepherd, hired by another man, and I do not profit from the sheep that I watch. My master is a mean-spirited man and does not care about finding a path to heaven through good works of hospitality. Besides, his house, his flocks, and his feed for the sheep are all on sale, and so at the cottage, since he is gone, there is nothing to eat. But whatever is there you can have, come and see what is left. You are most welcome.*

ROSALIND
What is he that shall buy his flock and pasture?

Who is buying his flock and pasture?

CORIN
That young swain that you saw here but erewhile,
That little cares for buying any thing.

*The young man whom you saw here a moment ago,
though he doesn't really about buying anything.*

ROSALIND
I pray thee, if it stand with honesty,
Buy thou the cottage, pasture and the flock,
And thou shalt have to pay for it of us.

*Please, if it can be done honestly,
buy the cottage, pasture, and flock for us,
and we will pay you for it.*

CELIA
And we will mend thy wages. I like this place.

We will also increase your wages. I like it this

And willingly could waste my time in it.

CORIN
Assuredly the thing is to be sold:
Go with me: if you like upon report
The soil, the profit and this kind of life,
I will your very faithful feeder be
And buy it with your gold right suddenly.

place and can would like to waste my time here.

Truly, the place is going to be sold.
Come with me and if you like how the soil looks,
and the profit you think can be had, and this
way of life, then I will be a faithful servant and
will buy it with your money right away.

Exeunt

SCENE V. The Forest.

Enter AMIENS, JAQUES, and others.

AMIENS
singing
Under the greenwood tree
Who loves to lie with me,
And turn his merry note
Unto the sweet bird's throat,
Come hither, come hither, come hither:
Here shall he see No enemy
But winter and rough weather.

Under the greenwood tree
whoever wants to lie with me
and sing the song
that comes from the sweet bird's throat,
come here, come here, come here.
Here there will be no enemy
except winter and rough weather.

JAQUES
More, more, I prithee, more.

More, more, please, sing more.

AMIENS
It will make you melancholy, Monsieur Jaques.

It will make you sad, Mister Jacques.

JAQUES
I thank it. More, I prithee, more. I can suck
melancholy out of a song, as a weasel sucks
eggs.
More, I prithee, more.

I welcome it. Please, sing more. I can suck
sadness from a song like a weasel can suck
eggs.
Sing more, please.

AMIENS
My voice is ragged: I know I cannot please you.

My voice is strained – I can't please you now.

JAQUES
I do not desire you to please me; I do desire you
to
sing. Come, more; another stanzo: call you 'em
stanzos?

I don't want you to please me; I want you to
sing. Come on, just one more sstanza – are they
called stanzas?

AMIENS
What you will, Monsieur Jaques.

You can call them whatever you want, Monsieur
Jacques.

JAQUES
Nay, I care not for their names; they owe me
nothing. Will you sing?

No, I don't care to know their names. They don't
owe me anything. Will you sing?

AMIENS
More at your request than to please myself.

Only because you are asking for it, and not out

JAQUES
Well then, if ever I thank any man, I'll thank you;
but that they call compliment is like the encounter
of two dog-apes, and when a man thanks me heartily,
methinks I have given him a penny and he renders me
the beggarly thanks. Come, sing; and you that will
not, hold your tongues.

AMIENS
Well, I'll end the song. Sirs, cover the while; the duke will drink under this tree. He hath been all this day to look you.

JAQUES
And I have been all this day to avoid him. He is too disputable for my company: I think of as many
matters as he, but I give heaven thanks and make no
boast of them. Come, warble, come.

Everyone sings
Who doth ambition shun
And loves to live i' the sun,
Seeking the food he eats
And pleased with what he gets,
Come hither, come hither, come hither:
Here shall he see No enemy
But winter and rough weather.

JAQUES
I'll give you a verse to this note that I made yesterday in despite of my invention.

AMIENS
And I'll sing it.

JAQUES
Thus it goes:--
If it do come to pass

of pleasure.

Then if I ever thank someone, I thank you most. But to compliment another man is awkward, like two baboons meeting – when another man thanks me,
I feel like I have given him a penny and that he has
become a beggar. Now, sing, and whoever will not sing, be quiet.

Well, I will finish the song. Men, while I am doing this, set the table, since
the duke will drink under this tree. He has been looking all day for you, Jacques.

And I have been avoiding him all day. He is too argumentative for me. I think about as many things as he does, but I give thanks for the thoughts, and do not
talk about them in front of others. Come, sing for me.

Whoever shuns ambition
and loves to live in the sun,
hunting for food to eat
and happy with whatever he finds,
come here, come here, come here.
Here there are no enemies
except winter and rough weather.

I will give you a verse to sing to this tune that I made up
yesterday, though it is not too imaginative.

I'll sing it.

It goes like this:
If it comes to pass

That any man turn ass,
Leaving his wealth and ease,
A stubborn will to please,
Ducdame, ducdame, ducdame:
Here shall he see
Gross fools as he,
An if he will come to me.

that a man becomes an ass,
leaving his wealth and ease of life
because he wants to please his stubborn will,
ducdame, ducdame, ducdame.
Here he will see
fools as disgusting as he is,
as long as he will come to me.

AMIENS
What's that 'ducdame'?

What does "ducdame" mean?

JAQUES
'Tis a Greek invocation, to call fools into a circle. I'll go sleep, if I can; if I cannot, I'll rail against all the first-born of Egypt.

It is a Greek word used to call fools into a circle. I will go to sleep if I can – if I can't, I'll yell at all of the first-born in Egypt.

AMIENS
And I'll go seek the duke: his banquet is prepared.

I will go look for the duke, his banquet is ready.

Exeunt severally

SCENE VI. The forest.

Enter ORLANDO and ADAM

ADAM

Dear master, I can go no further. O, I die for
food!
Here lie I down, and measure out my grave.
Farewell,
kind master.

*Master, I can't go further. O I am dying of
hunger!
Here will I lie in order to measure a plot for my
grave. Goodbye,
kind master.*

ORLANDO

Why, how now, Adam! no greater heart in thee?
Live
a little; comfort a little; cheer thyself a little.
If this uncouth forest yield any thing savage, I
will either be food for it or bring it for food to
thee. Thy conceit is nearer death than thy
powers.
For my sake be comfortable; hold death awhile
at
the arm's end: I will here be with thee presently;
and if I bring thee not something to eat, I will
give thee leave to die: but if thou diest before I
come, thou art a mocker of my labour. Well
said!
thou lookest cheerly, and I'll be with thee
quickly.
Yet thou liest in the bleak air: come, I will bear
thee to some shelter; and thou shalt not die for
lack of a dinner, if there live any thing in this
desert. Cheerly, good Adam!

*Well now, Adam! Do you have no greater
strength than this? Live
a little, be comforted a little, and cheer up a
little.
If any savage thing comes from this rude forest,
I will either become its food , or I will bring it
as food for
you. You think you are nearer to death that you
reall are.
For my sake, be comfortable. Keep death at
an arm's length away and I will be back soon.
If I do not bring you anything to eat, then you
will have permission to die, but if you die before
I return, you are mocking my hard work. There!
You look well, and I will be back wuickly.
But, right now you lie in the open air. Come and
I will carry
you to shelter. You will not die from
hunger, as long as there is something living in
this deserted place. Be happy, good Adam!*

Exeunt

SCENE VII. The forest.

A table set out. Enter DUKE SENIOR, AMIENS, and Lords like outlaws

DUKE SENIOR
I think he be transform'd into a beast;
For I can no where find him like a man.

I think he must have transformed into an animal because I cannot find him as a man anywhere I look.

First Lord
My lord, he is but even now gone hence:
Here was he merry, hearing of a song.

My lord, he left only recently.
He was here, happy, listening to a song.

DUKE SENIOR
If he, compact of jars, grow musical,
We shall have shortly discord in the spheres.
Go, seek him: tell him I would speak with him.

If he, packed tight with conflict, becomes musical, than there will be something wrong in the heavens. Go and find him, and tell him that I wish to speak with him.

Enter JAQUES

First Lord
He saves my labour by his own approach.

I don't have to, since he has come on his own.

DUKE SENIOR
Why, how now, monsieur! what a life is this,
That your poor friends must woo your
company?
What, you look merrily!

How are you, monsieur! What kind of life is this when your poor friends have to beg you for your company?
You look happy!

JAQUES
A fool, a fool! I met a fool i' the forest,
A motley fool; a miserable world!
As I do live by food, I met a fool
Who laid him down and bask'd him in the sun,
And rail'd on Lady Fortune in good terms,
In good set terms and yet a motley fool.
'Good morrow, fool,' quoth I. 'No, sir,' quoth he,
'Call me not fool till heaven hath sent me
fortune:'
And then he drew a dial from his poke,
And, looking on it with lack-lustre eye,
Says very wisely, 'It is ten o'clock:
Thus we may see,' quoth he, 'how the world
wags:
'Tis but an hour ago since it was nine,

A fool! I met a clown in the forest wearing his motley costume. What a miserable world! As surely as I eat food to live, I met a clown who laid himself down to bask in the sun and cursed Lady Fortune jokingly, in clever words, though still surely a clown.
"Good day, fool," I said. "No, sir," he replied, "Do not call me a fool until heaven has sent me a fortune."
Then he pulled a watch from his bag and, looking on it with a dim eye, said wisely, "It is ten o'clock: and thus we can see how the world moves. Only an hour ago it was nine, and an hour later it will be eleven.
And after one hour more 'twill be eleven;

And so, from hour to hour, we ripe and ripe,
And then, from hour to hour, we rot and rot;
And thereby hangs a tale.' When I did hear
The motley fool thus moral on the time,
My lungs began to crow like chanticleer,
That fools should be so deep-contemplative,
And I did laugh sans intermission
An hour by his dial. O noble fool!
A worthy fool! Motley's the only wear.

DUKE SENIOR
What fool is this?

JAQUES
O worthy fool! One that hath been a courtier,
And says, if ladies be but young and fair,
They have the gift to know it: and in his brain,
Which is as dry as the remainder biscuit
After a voyage, he hath strange places cramm'd
With observation, the which he vents
In mangled forms. O that I were a fool!
I am ambitious for a motley coat.

DUKE SENIOR
Thou shalt have one.

JAQUES
It is my only suit;
Provided that you weed your better judgments
Of all opinion that grows rank in them
That I am wise. I must have liberty
Withal, as large a charter as the wind,
To blow on whom I please; for so fools have;
And they that are most galled with my folly,
They most must laugh. And why, sir, must they so?
The 'why' is plain as way to parish church:
He that a fool doth very wisely hit
Doth very foolishly, although he smart,
Not to seem senseless of the bob: if not,
The wise man's folly is anatomized
Even by the squandering glances of the fool.
Invest me in my motley; give me leave
To speak my mind, and I will through and through

And so on, from hour to hour, we grow and we ripen, and then, from hour to hour, we get old, and we rot,
and there is a story to that." When I heard this motley wearing fool moralize time, I crowed and laughed like a rooster, that clowns should be so contemplative. I laughed without pause an hour by his watch. O noble fool! A worthy clown! Motley is the only thing he should wear.

What fool is this?

A worthy one! He used to be a courtier and said "If ladies are young and beautiful, they always know it." In his brain, which is dry like a biscuit on a ship and thus not impressed by much, are strange facts and crammed in observations, which he speaks in twisted ways. O if I were a clown!

You could be one.

That is my only case, as long as then you remove any judgments and opinions that you have that I am wise. I must have freedom, as much as the wind gets, to blow on and mock whomever I please, just as clowns may. They that are most offended by my jokes must laugh hardest. And why is that? Well that is as plain as the path to a small country church: whoever a fool wisely makes fun of would be acting very foolishly, though otherwise smart, if he didn't act like the joke didn't affect him. If he didn't, then the foolish action of the wise man would be seen and scrutinized by even the silly work of the clown. Give me a motley costume, and give me permission to speak my mind, and I will,

Cleanse the foul body of the infected world,
If they will patiently receive my medicine.

DUKE SENIOR
Fie on thee! I can tell what thou wouldst do.

JAQUES
What, for a counter, would I do but good?

DUKE SENIOR
Most mischievous foul sin, in chiding sin:
For thou thyself hast been a libertine,
As sensual as the brutish sting itself;
And all the embossed sores and headed evils,
That thou with licence of free foot hast caught,
Wouldst thou disgorge into the general world.

JAQUES
Why, who cries out on pride,
That can therein tax any private party?
Doth it not flow as hugely as the sea,
Till that the weary very means do ebb?
What woman in the city do I name,
When that I say the city-woman bears
The cost of princes on unworthy shoulders?
Who can come in and say that I mean her,
When such a one as she such is her neighbour?
Or what is he of basest function
That says his bravery is not of my cost,
Thinking that I mean him, but therein suits
His folly to the mettle of my speech?
There then; how then? what then? Let me see wherein
My tongue hath wrong'd him: if it do him right,
Then he hath wrong'd himself; if he be free,
Why then my taxing like a wild-goose flies,
Unclaim'd of any man. But who comes here?

ORLANDO
Forbear, and eat no more.

JAQUES
Why, I have eat none yet.

through and through clean the sick body of the infections surrounding it, as long as my patients will patiently take the medicine I give them.

Curse you! I know what you would do.

What would I do except good things?

A most evil, disgusting sin, by rebuking sin. You yourself have been a rake and a lecher, as lustful as the sting of lust itself. And now, all of the diseased sores and evils that you in your freedom caught, you want to find in others in the whole world.

But, if I speak out against pride, am I singling out some individual? Or rather does pride flow as greatly as the sea itself, until it wearily reaches the very edges of the sea? What woman in the city have I named when I say that the city-woman wears clothes that cost princely amounts on her unworthy shoulders? Who can come to me and say that I am talking about her when her neighbors are just like she is? And who is that base coward who says that his bravery is not my concern, thinking that I talk about him: doesn't he claim his own foolishness by thinking that I do? Well, then how? And now what? Show me where I have spoken wrong of him. If my words end up rebuking him, then he was wrong in the first place, and if he is free from such rebuke, then my words fly away like wild geese, owned by no man. Who is it that is coming?

Enter ORLANDO, with his sword drawn

Stop, and don't eat anything more.

But I have not eaten anything yet.

52

ORLANDO

Nor shalt not, till necessity be served.

And you won't, until what I need is served.

JAQUES

Of what kind should this cock come of?

What kind of fighting rooster is this?

DUKE SENIOR

Art thou thus bolden'd, man, by thy distress,
Or else a rude despiser of good manners,
That in civility thou seem'st so empty?

*Is your boldness from distress
or because you are a rude man who despises
good manners,
that you seem so lacking of politeness.*

ORLANDO

You touch'd my vein at first: the thorny point
Of bare distress hath ta'en from me the show
Of smooth civility: yet am I inland bred
And know some nurture. But forbear, I say:
He dies that touches any of this fruit
Till I and my affairs are answered.

*You had it right with the first guess. The thorn
of my distress has taken from me my
smooth manners. Yet, I was bred in the city
and do know how to be civil. But stop, I say:
Whoever touched this fruit
until my affairs are answered will die.*

JAQUES

An you will not be answered with reason, I must die.

*If these affairs will not be answered with reason,
I will have to die.*

DUKE SENIOR

What would you have? Your gentleness shall force
More than your force move us to gentleness.

*What would you like? Being a gentleman would
force more from us than your force would make
us gentle.*

ORLANDO

I almost die for food; and let me have it.

I am dying from hunger – let me have it.

DUKE SENIOR

Sit down and feed, and welcome to our table.

Sit down and eat, and welcome to our table.

ORLANDO

Speak you so gently? Pardon me, I pray you:
I thought that all things had been savage here;
And therefore put I on the countenance
Of stern commandment. But whate'er you are
That in this desert inaccessible,
Under the shade of melancholy boughs,
Lose and neglect the creeping hours of time
If ever you have look'd on better days,
If ever been where bells have knoll'd to church,
If ever sat at any good man's feast,
If ever from your eyelids wiped a tear

*Why do you speak so nicely to me? Excuse me,
please. I thought that everything here was
savage, so I put on an act of sternness and
strength. But whoever you are in this
inaccessible and deserted place, where you sit
under the shade of sad trees and lose track of
the time, if you have ever known better days
or have been to church where the bells rang,
if you ever sat at a nobleman's feast, or if you
have ever wiped a tear from you eye and thus
know what it is like to pity and be pitied,*

And know what 'tis to pity and be pitied,
Let gentleness my strong enforcement be:
In the which hope I blush, and hide my sword.

*than let my manners be a strong persuader,
and in that hope I will feel ashamed and put my
sword away.*

DUKE SENIOR
True is it that we have seen better days,
And have with holy bell been knoll'd to church
And sat at good men's feasts and wiped our eyes
Of drops that sacred pity hath engender'd:
And therefore sit you down in gentleness
And take upon command what help we have
That to your wanting may be minister'd.

*It is true that we have seen better days
and have been to church where the bells rang
and have sat at noblemen's feasts and wiped our
eyes of tears that came from holy pity.
Therefore, sit down nicely
and take whatever help we have
that we can provide to your needs.*

ORLANDO
Then but forbear your food a little while,
Whiles, like a doe, I go to find my fawn
And give it food. There is an old poor man,
Who after me hath many a weary step
Limp'd in pure love: till he be first suffic'd,
Oppress'd with two weak evils, age and hunger,
I will not touch a bit.

*Then please stop eating for a moment
while I, like a doe, find my fawn
and give it food. A poor old man
has followed me in every tired step
and limped along from his love for me. Until he
is satisfied, since he is afflicted by two
weaknesses – age and hunger – I will not eat.*

DUKE SENIOR
Go find him out,
And we will nothing waste till you return.

*Go find him
and we will not eat until you return.*

ORLANDO
I thank ye; and be blest for your good comfort!

Thank you, and bless you for your hospitality!

Exit

DUKE SENIOR
Thou seest we are not all alone unhappy:
This wide and universal theatre
Presents more woeful pageants than the scene
Wherein we play in.

*You see, we are not all unhappy and alone:
this wide and universal theater
has more sad plays than only the scene
that we are in.*

JAQUES
All the world's a stage,
And all the men and women merely players:
They have their exits and their entrances;
And one man in his time plays many parts,
His acts being seven ages. At first the infant,
Mewling and puking in the nurse's arms.
And then the whining school-boy, with his
satchel

*The whole world is a stage
and men and women are just players.
They have their exits and entrances,
and one man plays many parts in his time,
seven different acts of live. First he is an infant,
crying and puking in the nurse's arms,
and then he is a whining schoolboy, with his bag
and his shining morning face, going as slow as a*

And shining morning face, creeping like snail
Unwillingly to school. And then the lover,
Sighing like furnace, with a woeful ballad
Made to his mistress' eyebrow. Then a soldier,
Full of strange oaths and bearded like the pard,
Jealous in honour, sudden and quick in quarrel,
Seeking the bubble reputation
Even in the cannon's mouth. And then the justice,
In fair round belly with good capon lined,
With eyes severe and beard of formal cut,
Full of wise saws and modern instances;
And so he plays his part. The sixth age shifts
Into the lean and slipper'd pantaloon,
With spectacles on nose and pouch on side,
His youthful hose, well saved, a world too wide
For his shrunk shank; and his big manly voice,
Turning again toward childish treble, pipes
And whistles in his sound. Last scene of all,
That ends this strange eventful history,
Is second childishness and mere oblivion,
Sans teeth, sans eyes, sans taste, sans everything.

DUKE SENIOR
Welcome. Set down your venerable burthen,
And let him feed.

ORLANDO
I thank you most for him.

ADAM
So had you need:
I scarce can speak to thank you for myself.

DUKE SENIOR
Welcome; fall to: I will not trouble you
As yet, to question you about your fortunes.
Give us some music; and, good cousin, sing.

AMIENS
singing
Blow, blow, thou winter wind.
Thou art not so unkind
As man's ingratitude;

*snail
to school, unwillingly. Then he is a lover,
sighing like a furnace and singing sad songs
about his mistress's eyebrow. Then he is a
soldier, swearing strangely and bearded like a
panther jealous of his honor and quick to fight,
looking for his reputation, as fragile as a
bubble, even looking in the mouth of a cannon.
Then he is a judge,
with a fat belly full of chicken,
and serious eyes, and a formally trimmed beard,
full of wise sayings and relevant stories –
that's how he plays this part. In the sixth part,
he is a thin and slipper-wearing old fool,
with glasses on his nose and a bag at his side,
his stockings from his youth, still saved, droop
on his shrunken legs and his formerly manly
voice returns to childish sounds and whistles.
Finally,
the scene that ends this strange and storied
history, is a second childhood, one he doesn't
even know about, without teeth or eyes or taste,
without anything.*

Re-enter ORLANDO, with ADAM

*Welcome. Sit down your respectable burden
and let him eat.*

I will thank you for him.

*You must –
I can barely speak to thank you for myself.*

*Welcome, and go ahead. I will not bother you
yet and question how you came here.
Someone play some music, and good cousin,
please sing.*

*Blow, blow, you winter wind.
You are not as mean
as men's ingratitude,*

Thy tooth is not so keen,
Because thou art not seen,
Although thy breath be rude.
Heigh-ho! sing, heigh-ho! unto the green holly:
Most friendship is feigning, most loving mere folly:
Then, heigh-ho, the holly!
This life is most jolly.
Freeze, freeze, thou bitter sky,
That dost not bite so nigh
As benefits forgot:
Though thou the waters warp,
Thy sting is not so sharp
As friend remember'd not.
Heigh-ho! sing, heigh-ho! unto the green holly:
Most friendship is feigning, most loving mere folly:
Then, heigh-ho, the holly!

DUKE SENIOR
If that you were the good Sir Rowland's son,
As you have whisper'd faithfully you were,
And as mine eye doth his effigies witness
Most truly limn'd and living in your face,
Be truly welcome hither: I am the duke
That loved your father: the residue of your fortune,
Go to my cave and tell me. Good old man,
Thou art right welcome as thy master is.
Support him by the arm. Give me your hand,
And let me all your fortunes understand.

*and your teeth aren't as sharp
since you are invisible –
though your breath is rude and harsh.
Sing, Heigh-ho, Heigh-ho! to the green holly.
Most friendship is fake, most love is a joke.
Sing, Heigh-ho, the holly!
This life is very happy.
Freeze, freeze, you bitter sky,
your bite is not as bad
as forgotten good deeds.
Though you can shape water by freezing it,
your sting is not as bad
as friend who is not remembered.
Sing, Heigh-ho, Heigh-ho! to the green holly.
Most friendship is fake, most love is a joke.
Sing, Heigh-ho, the holly!*

*If you are really Sir Rowland's son –
as you have faithfully whispered to me,
and as I witness in your physical likeness to him
most obviously in your facial details –
you truly are welcome here. I am the duke
who loved your father, the relation to your fortune.
Come to my cave and talk to me. Good old man,
you are just as welcome as your master.
Hold onto him by the arm. Give me your hand
and tell me everything that has happened to you.*

Exeunt

56

Act III

SCENE I. A room in the palace.

Enter DUKE FREDERICK, Lords, and OLIVER

DUKE FREDERICK
Not see him since? Sir, sir, that cannot be:
But were I not the better part made mercy,
I should not seek an absent argument
Of my revenge, thou present. But look to it:
Find out thy brother, wheresoe'er he is;
Seek him with candle; bring him dead or living
Within this twelvemonth, or turn thou no more
To seek a living in our territory.
Thy lands and all things that thou dost call thine
Worth seizure do we seize into our hands,
Till thou canst quit thee by thy brother's mouth
Of what we think against thee.

*You haven't seen him since? Sir, that can't be.
If I were not made mostly of mercy,
then I would not carry out my argument against
someone who is absent but would take my
revenge on you, being present. See to it:
find out wherever your brother is, look for him
even by night with a candle, and bring him dead
or alive within the next year, or do not return
to live in this country. Your lands, and
everything you call your own that is valuable,
we will seize until by your brother's testimony
you are removed from the guilt I think you have.*

OLIVER
O that your highness knew my heart in this!
I never loved my brother in my life.

*O if only your highness knew how I thought
about this in my heart!
I have never loved my brother in my whole life.*

DUKE FREDERICK
More villain thou. Well, push him out of doors;
And let my officers of such a nature
Make an extent upon his house and lands:
Do this expediently and turn him going.

*You are a bigger villain then. Push him through
the doors and let my officers
seize his house and lands.
Do this quickly and make him leave.*

Exeunt

SCENE II. The forest.

ORLANDO
Hang there, my verse, in witness of my love:
And thou, thrice-crowned queen of night, survey
With thy chaste eye, from thy pale sphere above,
Thy huntress' name that my full life doth sway.
O Rosalind! these trees shall be my books
And in their barks my thoughts I'll character;
That every eye which in this forest looks
Shall see thy virtue witness'd every where.
Run, run, Orlando; carve on every tree
The fair, the chaste and unexpressive she.

Sit here on this tree, you lines of poetry, to witness to my love. And you, Diana, queen of the night, watch with your pure eye from the pale moon above and keep track of the huntress who has power over my life. O Rosalind! These trees will be my books and I will write my thoughts for you on their bark; thus, everyone who looks in this forest will see your virtues written everywhere. Run, Orlando, and carve lines on every tree that talk about her beauty, chastity, and her inexpressible character.

Exit
Enter CORIN and TOUCHSTONE

CORIN
And how like you this shepherd's life, Master
Touchstone?

How do you like living as a shepherd, Master Touchstone?

TOUCHSTONE
Truly, shepherd, in respect of itself, it is a good
life, but in respect that it is a shepherd's life,
it is naught. In respect that it is solitary, I
like it very well; but in respect that it is
private, it is a very vile life. Now, in respect it
is in the fields, it pleaseth me well; but in
respect it is not in the court, it is tedious. As
is it a spare life, look you, it fits my humour
well;
but as there is no more plenty in it, it goes much
against my stomach. Hast any philosophy in
thee, shepherd?

Well, shepherd, compared to itself alone, it is a good life, but since it is a shepherd's life, it is nothing. In respect of its solitary lifestyle, I like it a lot, but in respect of its private lifestyle, it is awful. Now, it is pleasing to live in the fields, but it is very boring and tedious to not be living in the courts. And with its minimal needs, it is very fitting to my personality, but because there is no extravagance, the lifestyle goes against my palate and dietary desires. Are you a philosopher, shepherd?

CORIN
No more but that I know the more one sickens
the
worse at ease he is; and that he that wants
money,
means and content is without three good friends;
that the property of rain is to wet and fire to
burn; that good pasture makes fat sheep, and

Only insofar as I know that the sicker one gets, the more uncomfortable he is, and that if someone does not have money, means of employment, or happiness is lacking three good friends. I know that rain gets things wet, and fire burns, that good fields make fat

that a
great cause of the night is lack of the sun; that
he that hath learned no wit by nature nor art may
complain of good breeding or comes of a very
dull kindred.

sheep, and that
the great work of the night is to be without sun. I
know that he who has learned nothing, either
from nature or schooling, is either poorly bred
or has come from a dull family.

TOUCHSTONE
Such a one is a natural philosopher. Wast ever in
court, shepherd?

So you are a natural philosopher. Were you ever
in the court, shepherd?

CORIN
No, truly.

No, never.

TOUCHSTONE
Then thou art damned.

Then you are damned.

CORIN
Nay, I hope.

No, I hope not.

TOUCHSTONE
Truly, thou art damned like an ill-roasted egg, all
on one side.

Yes, you are damned like a poorly cooked egg,
all
burnt on one side.

CORIN
For not being at court? Your reason.

Just for never being at the court? Why? Tell me
your reasons.

TOUCHSTONE
Why, if thou never wast at court, thou never
sawest
good manners; if thou never sawest good
manners,
then thy manners must be wicked; and
wickedness is
sin, and sin is damnation. Thou art in a parlous
state, shepherd.

If you were never at the court, then you never
saw
good manners, and if you never saw good
manners,
then your manners must be wicked and bad, and
wickedness is
a sin, and sin is damnation. You are in a
perilous, dangerous state, shepherd.

CORIN
Not a whit, Touchstone: those that are good
manners
at the court are as ridiculous in the country as
the
behavior of the country is most mockable at the
court. You told me you salute not at the court,
but

Not at all, Touchstone: the good manners
of the court are just as ridiculous here in the
country as the
behavior of those from the country is made fun
of in the
court. You told me that one does not salute in
the court, but

you kiss your hands: that courtesy would be
uncleanly, if courtiers were shepherds.

TOUCHSTONE
Instance, briefly; come, instance.

CORIN
Why, we are still handling our ewes, and their
fells, you know, are greasy.

TOUCHSTONE
Why, do not your courtier's hands sweat? and is
not
the grease of a mutton as wholesome as the
sweat of
a man? Shallow, shallow. A better instance, I
say; come.

CORIN
Besides, our hands are hard.

TOUCHSTONE
Your lips will feel them the sooner. Shallow
again.
A more sounder instance, come.

CORIN
And they are often tarred over with the surgery
of
our sheep: and would you have us kiss tar? The
courtier's hands are perfumed with civet.

TOUCHSTONE
Most shallow man! thou worms-meat, in respect
of a
good piece of flesh indeed! Learn of the wise,
and
perpend: civet is of a baser birth than tar, the
very uncleanly flux of a cat. Mend the instance,
shepherd.

CORIN
You have too courtly a wit for me: I'll rest.

TOUCHSTONE
Wilt thou rest damned? God help thee, shallow

*instead kisses hands – that would be
very dirty if court members were shepherds.*

Quickly, give an example.

*Well we are handling sheep always, and their
fleece is, as you know, greasy.*

*Doesn't a court member's hands sweat? And
isn't
sheep's grease better than the sweat of
a man? That is a shallow reason – come up with
a better one. Come on.*

Also, our hands are hard.

*Your lips will still feel them. Another bad
reason. Come up with a sounder one, come on.*

*They are also often tarred from the tar we put
on the sheep to heal their wounds – would you
want to kiss tar? The
court member's hands are perfumed with civet
musk.*

*O shallow man! You are as worthless as worms-
meat compared
to a good steak! Learn from the wise and
understand this: civet musk is much worse than
tar –
it's the disgusting discharge from a cat. A better
example, shepherd.*

Your wit is too courtly for me – I will stop.

You are stopping even though you are still

man!
God make incision in thee! thou art raw.

damned? God help you, you shallow man!
God cut into you like a surgeon! You need aid.

CORIN
Sir, I am a true labourer: I earn that I eat, get
that I wear, owe no man hate, envy no man's
happiness, glad of other men's good, content
with my
harm, and the greatest of my pride is to see my
ewes
graze and my lambs suck.

*Sir, I am an honest and simple worker: I earn
what I eat, get
what I wear, hate no man, do not envy anyone's
happiness, am happy at others' good fortunes,
am content with my
own poor fortune, and my greatest pride is to
watch my ewes
graze and feed, and the lambs give suck.*

TOUCHSTONE
That is another simple sin in you, to bring the
ewes
and the rams together and to offer to get your
living by the copulation of cattle; to be bawd to
a
bell-wether, and to betray a she-lamb of a
twelvemonth to a crooked-pated, old, cuckoldly
ram,
out of all reasonable match. If thou beest not
damned for this, the devil himself will have no
shepherds; I cannot see else how thou shouldst
'scape.

*That is just another of your simple sins: you
bring the ewes
and rams together and you make your
living by their copulation. You are a pimp for
the rams, and you betray ewes, only a
year old, to crooked, old, unfaithful rams –
a disgusting match. If you are not
damned for this, then the devil himself must not
want
shepherds in Hell. I don't see how else you will
escape.*

CORIN
Here comes young Master Ganymede, my new
mistress's brother.

*Here comes Master Ganymede, my new
mistress's brother.*

Enter ROSALIND, with a paper, reading

ROSALIND
reading
From the east to western Ind,
No jewel is like Rosalind.
Her worth, being mounted on the wind,
Through all the world bears Rosalind.
All the pictures fairest lined
Are but black to Rosalind.
Let no fair be kept in mind
But the fair of Rosalind.

*From the east, to the western Indies,
no jewel compares to Rosalind.
Her worth is carried by the wind
that tells the whole world of Rosalind.
All of the most beautifully drawn pictures
look like black marks next to Rosalind.
Let nothing valuable be in one's mind
except the beauty of Rosalind.*

TOUCHSTONE
I'll rhyme you so eight years together, dinners
and

*I can rhyme like that for eight years straight,
dinners, other meals, and time for sleep*

suppers and sleeping-hours excepted: it is the
right butter-women's rank to market.

ROSALIND
Out, fool!

TOUCHSTONE
For a taste:
If a hart do lack a hind,
Let him seek out Rosalind.
If the cat will after kind,
So be sure will Rosalind.
Winter garments must be lined,
So must slender Rosalind.
They that reap must sheaf and bind;
Then to cart with Rosalind.
Sweetest nut hath sourest rind,
Such a nut is Rosalind.
He that sweetest rose will find
Must find love's prick and Rosalind.
This is the very false gallop of verses: why do you
infect yourself with them?

ROSALIND
Peace, you dull fool! I found them on a tree.

TOUCHSTONE
Truly, the tree yields bad fruit.

ROSALIND
I'll graff it with you, and then I shall graff it
with a medlar: then it will be the earliest fruit
i' the country; for you'll be rotten ere you be half
ripe, and that's the right virtue of the medlar.

TOUCHSTONE
You have said; but whether wisely or no, let the
forest judge.

ROSALIND
Peace! Here comes my sister, reading: stand
aside.

excepted: it is as bad and easy as a common-woman's path to the market.

Get out, fool!

I'll show you:
If a buck lacks a doe,
let him look for Rosalind.
If the cat goes after its own kind,
so too does Rosalind.
Winter clothes must be lined for warmth,
and Rosalind needs something around her, too.
Farmers that reap must then sheaf and bind the
crops, So add Rosalind to the harvest cart.
The sweetest nut has the sourest rind,
Just like Rosalind.
He who finds the sweetest rose,
will also be pricked by thorns of love and
Rosalind. This is how poor and simple the meter
of these verses are – why are you
infecting yourself by repeating them?

Be quiet, you dumb fool! I found them written on
a tree.

Then such a tree is giving off bad fruit.

I will graft you onto it, and then it will be
grafted with fruit that is ripe after it becomes
rotten. You will be the first fruit to ripen in the
country because you will be rotten before you
ever get half
ripe – and that's the way medlar fruits grow.

So you say, but the forest will judge whether you
are right or not.

Enter CELIA, with a writing

Be quiet! Here comes my sister, reading.

CELIA

[Reads]

Why should this a desert be?
For it is unpeopled? No:
Tongues I'll hang on every tree,
That shall civil sayings show:
Some, how brief the life of man
Runs his erring pilgrimage,
That the stretching of a span
Buckles in his sum of age;
Some, of violated vows
'Twixt the souls of friend and friend:
But upon the fairest boughs,
Or at every sentence end,
Will I Rosalinda write,
Teaching all that read to know
The quintessence of every sprite
Heaven would in little show.
Therefore Heaven Nature charged
That one body should be fill'd
With all graces wide-enlarged:
Nature presently distill'd
Helen's cheek, but not her heart,
Cleopatra's majesty,
Atalanta's better part,
Sad Lucretia's modesty.
Thus Rosalind of many parts
By heavenly synod was devised,
Of many faces, eyes and hearts,
To have the touches dearest prized.
Heaven would that she these gifts should have,
And I to live and die her slave.

Should this be a desert just because there are no people? No, for I will give tongues to every tree so they will speak civilized things. Some will be about the brief life of man and how it is spent in a wrong journey, how his stretched out hand holds all of his years of life. Some will be about broken promises between friends. But on the best branches or at the end of every sentence I will write "Rosalinda" to teach everyone who reads the trees to know what the essence of every angel heaven shows in her. Heaven tasked Nature to make one person filled with all the beauties of womankind, so Nature combined Helen of Troy's cheek, but not her unfaithful heart, Cleopatra's majesty, the best parts of Atalanta, and sad Lucretia's modesty and purity. Thus, Rosalind was from many perfect parts by Heaven's order made: made from many faces, eyes, and hearts in order to have the most beautiful parts of all of them. Heaven decided that she should have these gifts and that I should live and die as her servant.

ROSALIND

O most gentle pulpiter! what tedious homily of love
have you wearied your parishioners withal, and never
cried 'Have patience, good people!'

O good preacher! What tiresome sermon of love you have been exhausting your congregation with, without warning them by saying, "Be patient!"?

CELIA

How now! back, friends! Shepherd, go off a little.
Go with him, sirrah.

What is that? Go back, friends! Shepherd, move away a little, and go with him, Touchstone.

TOUCHSTONE
Come, shepherd, let us make an honourable retreat;
though not with bag and baggage, yet with scrip and scrippage.

Come, shepherd, let's retreat honorably and leave –
not with a the baggage of an army, but with your shepherd's bag and what little we have.

Exeunt CORIN and TOUCHSTONE

CELIA
Didst thou hear these verses?

Did you hear the verses I read?

ROSALIND
O, yes, I heard them all, and more too; for some of
them had in them more feet than the verses would bear.

Yes, I heard all of them – even more than them. In fact,
some of the verses had too many syllables and feet for the rhyme scheme.

CELIA
That's no matter: the feet might bear the verses.

That's not important: extra feet can hold the verses better then.

ROSALIND
Ay, but the feet were lame and could not bear themselves without the verse and therefore stood lamely in the verse.

Yes, but the feet were lame – they were made of bad poetry – and could not hold themselves without the rhyme scheme; therefore they read weakly within the verse.

CELIA
But didst thou hear without wondering how thy name
should be hanged and carved upon these trees?

But did you listen to all of that without thinking about why your name should be written on all of the trees?

ROSALIND
I was seven of the nine days out of the wonder before you came; for look here what I found on a
palm-tree. I was never so be-rhymed since Pythagoras' time, that I was an Irish rat, which I can hardly remember.

I was already mostly through my thinking of them before you came. Look, I found others on a palm-tree. I wasn't rhymed about like this since a past life of mine when I was an Irish rat and poets thought they could rid me through verse, and I don't remember that.

CELIA
Trow you who hath done this?

Do you know who wrote all of this?

ROSALIND
Is it a man?

Is it a man?

CELIA
And a chain, that you once wore, about his neck. Change you colour?

Yes, one who has a chain, which you once wore, around his neck. Are you blushing?

ROSALIND

I prithee, who?

Tell me, who?

CELIA

O Lord, Lord! it is a hard matter for friends to
meet; but mountains may be removed with
earthquakes
and so encounter.

*O God! It is hard enough for two friends to
meet – but even mountains can be moved by
earthquakes
and forced into each other.*

ROSALIND

Nay, but who is it?

No, who is it?

CELIA

Is it possible?

Is it possible?

ROSALIND

Nay, I prithee now with most petitionary
vehemence,
tell me who it is.

*No, please, I'm begging you as strongly as I
can,
tell me who it is.*

CELIA

O wonderful, wonderful, and most wonderful
wonderful! and yet again wonderful, and after
that,
out of all hooping!

*O wonderful, wonderful, wonderful!
Yet again, wonderful, and even now,
when you are out of the hoop-skirts and dressed
like a man!*

ROSALIND

Good my complexion! dost thou think, though I
am
caparisoned like a man, I have a doublet and
hose in
my disposition? One inch of delay more is a
South-sea of discovery; I prithee, tell me who is
it
quickly, and speak apace. I would thou couldst
stammer, that thou mightst pour this concealed
man
out of thy mouth, as wine comes out of a
narrow-
mouthed bottle, either too much at once, or none
at
all. I prithee, take the cork out of thy mouth that
may drink thy tidings.

*Good heavens! Do you think that since I am
dressed like a man, manly attitudes carry over
to my character? One more second of delay is
as arduous
as journeying through the South Seas. Please,
tell me who it is
quickly, and speak to me. I wish that you could
stutter, and that then you would reveal the name
of this man
like pouring wine from a narrow-
mouthed bottle, either all at once or not at
all. Please, remove the cork from your mouth so
that
I can drink your words.*

CELIA

So you may put a man in your belly.

And then you can put the man in your stomach.

ROSALIND
Is he of God's making? What manner of man? Is his
head worth a hat, or his chin worth a beard?

Did God make him? What kind of man is he? Does he
wear a hat? Does he have a beard?

CELIA
Nay, he hath but a little beard.

No, only a small beard.

ROSALIND
Why, God will send more, if the man will be
thankful: let me stay the growth of his beard, if
thou delay me not the knowledge of his chin.

Well God will give him a more full beard, if the
man thanks Him, and I will wait for the beard to
grow as long as you will not make me wait
longer to hear whose chin it grows on.

CELIA
It is young Orlando, that tripped up the wrestler's
heels and your heart both in an instant.

It is young Orlando, the man who defeated both
the wrestler
and your heart at once.

ROSALIND
Nay, but the devil take mocking: speak, sad brow and
true maid.

May the devil curse you for mocking me. Tell
me, be serious
and honest.

CELIA
I' faith, coz, 'tis he.

I swear, cousin, it is he.

ROSALIND
Orlando?

Orlando?

CELIA
Orlando.

Orlando.

ROSALIND
Alas the day! what shall I do with my doublet and
hose? What did he when thou sawest him? What said
he? How looked he? Wherein went he? What makes
him here? Did he ask for me? Where remains he?
How parted he with thee? and when shalt thou see
him again? Answer me in one word.

Oh no! What should I do with the men's clothing I
wear? What did he do when you saw him? What did he
say? How did he look? Where did he go? Why is
he here? Did he ask about me? Where is he
staying?
How did he leave you? When will you see
him again? Tell me with one word.

CELIA

You must borrow me Gargantua's mouth first:
'tis a
word too great for any mouth of this age's size.
To
say ay and no to these particulars is more than to
answer in a catechism.

*You must get me a giant's mouth first: that
word would be too large to fit in any human's
mouth. To
say yes and no to each question is more than
answering questions about Christian doctrine.*

ROSALIND

But doth he know that I am in this forest and in
man's apparel? Looks he as freshly as he did the
day he wrestled?

*Does he know that I am in the forest, and
dressed in men's clothing? Does he look as well
as he did on the day he wrestled?*

CELIA

It is as easy to count atomies as to resolve the
propositions of a lover; but take a taste of my
finding him, and relish it with good observance.
I found him under a tree, like a dropped acorn.

*It is easier to count atoms than to answer
every question of a lover. Taste my story of
finding him, and let that satisfy you through
your listening.*
I found him under a tree, like a dropped acorn.

ROSALIND

It may well be called Jove's tree, when it drops
forth such fruit.

*That sounds like a tree of God to drop
such wonderful fruit.*

CELIA

Give me audience, good madam.

Listen to me, good madam.

ROSALIND

Proceed.

Go on.

CELIA

There lay he, stretched along, like a wounded
knight.

*There he lay, stretched like he was a wounded
knight.*

ROSALIND

Though it be pity to see such a sight, it well
becomes the ground.

*It must have been a pitiful sight, but it also
must have been good for the ground to have him
on it.*

CELIA

Cry 'holla' to thy tongue, I prithee; it curvets
unseasonably. He was furnished like a hunter.

*Tell your tongue to stop, please, it gallops
against its reigns. He was dressed like a hunter.*

ROSALIND

O, ominous! he comes to kill my heart.

Oh no! He has come to kill my heart.

CELIA

I would sing my song without a burden: thou bringest
me out of tune.

ROSALIND
Do you not know I am a woman? when I think, I must
speak. Sweet, say on.

CELIA
You bring me out. Soft! comes he not here?

ROSALIND
'Tis he: slink by, and note him.

JAQUES
I thank you for your company; but, good faith, I had
as lief have been myself alone.

ORLANDO
And so had I; but yet, for fashion sake, I thank you
too for your society.

JAQUES
God be wi' you: let's meet as little as we can.

ORLANDO
I do desire we may be better strangers.

JAQUES
I pray you, mar no more trees with writing
love-songs in their barks.

ORLANDO
I pray you, mar no more of my verses with reading
them ill-favouredly.

JAQUES
Rosalind is your love's name?

ORLANDO

I would be singing my song easily, but you are forcing
me out of tune.

Don't you know that I am a woman? If I think something, I must
say it. Darling, continue.

You have made me lose track of my story. Quiet! Isn't that him?

Enter ORLANDO and JAQUES

It is he. Let's sneak by and watch him from hiding.

Thank you for your company, but honestly, I would
just as well be by myself.

So would I, but yet for politeness sake, Thank you
also for your company.

God be with you. Let us see each other as infrequently as possible.

I hope we can be better strangers.

Please, harm no more trees by writing love poems on their trunks.

Please, harm no more of my poems by reading them so antagonistically.

Is Rosalind your love's name?

Yes, just.

Yes, that is it.

JAQUES
I do not like her name.

I do not like her name.

ORLANDO
There was no thought of pleasing you when she was
christened.

No one thought of pleasing you when they named her.

JAQUES
What stature is she of?

How tall is she?

ORLANDO
Just as high as my heart.

She comes up to here – my heart.

JAQUES
You are full of pretty answers. Have you not been
acquainted with goldsmiths' wives, and conned them
out of rings?

You have many pretty answers. Are you well acquainted with goldsmiths' wives, and have memorized these answers from their rings where little poems are written?

ORLANDO
Not so; but I answer you right painted cloth, from
whence you have studied your questions.

No, but I answer you just like these noble tapestries from where you studied your questions.

JAQUES
You have a nimble wit: I think 'twas made of
Atalanta's heels. Will you sit down with me? and
we two will rail against our mistress the world and
all our misery.

You have a quick wit, perhaps made of Atalanta's heels. Will you sit with me? We can complain about the world, our true mistress, and all of our misery.

ORLANDO
I will chide no breather in the world but myself,
against whom I know most faults.

I will rebuke no human in the world except myself, since I know my faults best.

JAQUES
The worst fault you have is to be in love.

The worst fault is that you are in love.

ORLANDO
'Tis a fault I will not change for your best virtue.

That is a fault I will not change for the best

I am weary of you.

JAQUES
By my troth, I was seeking for a fool when I found
you.

ORLANDO
He is drowned in the brook: look but in, and you shall see him.

JAQUES
There I shall see mine own figure.

ORLANDO
Which I take to be either a fool or a cipher.

JAQUES
I'll tarry no longer with you: farewell, good
Signior Love.

ORLANDO
I am glad of your departure: adieu, good
Monsieur
Melancholy.

ROSALIND
[Aside to CELIA] I will speak to him, like a saucy
lackey and under that habit play the knave with him.
Do you hear, forester?

ORLANDO
Very well: what would you?

ROSALIND
I pray you, what is't o'clock?

ORLANDO
You should ask me what time o' day: there's no clock
in the forest.

ROSALIND

virtue. You are tiring me.

Honestly, I was looking for a fool when I found you.

The fool has drowned in the brook – stare in and you will see him.

I will only see myself.

Which is either a fool or a code.

I will wait on you no longer. Goodbye, Mister Love.

Your departure makes me happy. Goodbye Mister Sadness.

Exit JAQUES

I will speak to him, like an obnoxious boy, and under that character play a trick on him.
–Can you hear me, forester?

Very well: what do you want?

Please, what time is it?

You would be better off asking me what time of day it is – there is no time by the hour in the forest.

Then there is no true lover in the forest; else sighing every minute and groaning every hour would
detect the lazy foot of Time as well as a clock.

Then there is no true lover in the forest, or else he would by sighing every minute and groaning every hour mark the slow foot of Time like any clock.

ORLANDO
And why not the swift foot of Time? had not that
been as proper?

Why not the swift foot of Time? Isn't that more correct?

ROSALIND
By no means, sir: Time travels in divers paces with
divers persons. I'll tell you who Time ambles withal, who Time trots withal, who Time gallops
withal and who he stands still withal.

Not at all, sir. Time travels differently with different people. I can tell you whom Time walks with, whom Time jogs with, whom it gallops with, and whom he stands still with.

ORLANDO
I prithee, who doth he trot withal?

Tell me, whom does he jog with?

ROSALIND
Marry, he trots hard with a young maid between the
contract of her marriage and the day it is solemnized: if the interim be but a se'nnight, Time's pace is so hard that it seems the length of seven year.

Well, he jogs with a young maid who is between her engagement and the day of her marriage. If the interim time is only a week, Time still has such a pace that it always feels like seven years.

ORLANDO
Who ambles Time withal?

And who does it walk with?

ROSALIND
With a priest that lacks Latin and a rich man that hath not the gout, for the one sleeps easily because
he cannot study, and the other lives merrily because
he feels no pain, the one lacking the burden of lean
and wasteful learning, the other knowing no burden
of heavy tedious penury; these Time ambles withal.

With a priest who cannot read Latin, and a rich man who does not have the gout: one sleeps easily because he can't study Scripture and the other lives happily because he has no pain. The first lacks the burden of learning too much, and the second doesn't know the burden of heavy and wearying poverty. With these men Time walks.

ORLANDO
Who doth he gallop withal?

Whom does he gallop with?

ROSALIND
With a thief to the gallows, for though he go as
softly as foot can fall, he thinks himself too soon
there.

*With the thief on his way to the gallows, because
though he goes as slowly as feet can fall, he
always finds himself there too soon.*

ORLANDO
Who stays it still withal?

And who does it stand still with?

ROSALIND
With lawyers in the vacation, for they sleep
between
term and term and then they perceive not how
Time moves.

*With lawyers when they are on vacation,
because they just sleep
on their holidays and thus don't feel how Time
moves.*

ORLANDO
Where dwell you, pretty youth?

Where do you live, pretty young man?

ROSALIND
With this shepherdess, my sister; here in the
skirts of the forest, like fringe upon a petticoat.

*With the shepherdess here, my sister, on the
edge of the forest, like the fringe on a skirt.*

ORLANDO
Are you native of this place?

Are you a native here?

ROSALIND
As the cony that you see dwell where she is
kindled.

*As much as the rabbit who lives wherever she is
born.*

ORLANDO
Your accent is something finer than you could
purchase in so removed a dwelling.

*Your accent sounds finer than you could
get in such a distant home.*

ROSALIND
I have been told so of many: but indeed an old
religious uncle of mine taught me to speak, who
was
in his youth an inland man; one that knew
courtship
too well, for there he fell in love. I have heard
him read many lectures against it, and I thank
God
I am not a woman, to be touched with so many
giddy offences as he hath generally taxed their

*I have been told that by many before, but truly,
an old
religious uncle of mine taught me to speak, and
in
his youth he lived in the courts and knew
courtship
well – he even fell in love there. I have heard
him read many lectures against love, and I
thank God
I am not a woman, afflicted with*

whole sex withal.

ORLANDO
Can you remember any of the principal evils that he
laid to the charge of women?

ROSALIND
There were none principal; they were all like one
another as half-pence are, every one fault seeming
monstrous till his fellow fault came to match it.

ORLANDO
I prithee, recount some of them.

ROSALIND
No, I will not cast away my physic but on those that
are sick. There is a man haunts the forest, that
abuses our young plants with carving 'Rosalind' on
their barks; hangs odes upon hawthorns and elegies
on brambles, all, forsooth, deifying the name of
Rosalind: if I could meet that fancy-monger I would
give him some good counsel, for he seems to have the
quotidian of love upon him.

ORLANDO
I am he that is so love-shaked: I pray you tell me your remedy.

ROSALIND
There is none of my uncle's marks upon you: he
taught me how to know a man in love; in which cage
of rushes I am sure you are not prisoner.

ORLANDO
What were his marks?

all the giddiness that God has cursed their entire sex with.

Can you remember the primary evils that he blamed women for?

None were primary. They were all alike, like one half-pence coin is like another, and every fault seemed monstrous until the next one came along and was just as bad.

Please, tell me some of them.

No, I will not give away my medicine to anyone except those that are sick. There is a man who haunts this forest, abusing the young trees by carving "Rosalind" on the bark, hanging poems on the hawthorns and songs on the brambles, all, really, making holy the name of Rosalind. If I could meet that dreamer I would give him good counsel: he seems to be lovesick.

I am that man that is so torn by love. Please, tell me the remedy.

You don't seem to have any of my uncle's symptoms – he taught me how to know that a man is in love. In that cage I am sure you are not a prisoner.

What were his symptoms?

ROSALIND

A lean cheek, which you have not, a blue eye and
sunken, which you have not, an unquestionable
spirit, which you have not, a beard neglected,
which you have not; but I pardon you for that, for
simply your having in beard is a younger brother's
revenue: then your hose should be ungartered, your
bonnet unbanded, your sleeve unbuttoned, your shoe
untied and every thing about you demonstrating a
careless desolation; but you are no such man; you
are rather point-device in your accoutrements as
loving yourself than seeming the lover of any
other.

sunken in from not sleeping, which you don't have, a touchy,
quickly irritated mood, which you don't have, a messy beard,
which you don't have – but I will excuse that, since
your thin beard is telling of you being a younger man.
Your stockings should be loose, your
hat falling off, your sleeves unbuttoned, your shoes
untied, and everything about you showing
that you are carless in your dress from being so
upset. You are not such a man,
you are very well put-together in your dress, as
if you love yourself more than you seem to love anyone else.

ORLANDO

Fair youth, I would I could make thee believe I love.

Young man, I wish I could make you believe that I am in love.

ROSALIND

Me believe it! you may as soon make her that you
love believe it; which, I warrant, she is apter to
do than to confess she does: that is one of the
points in the which women still give the lie to
their consciences. But, in good sooth, are you he
that hangs the verses on the trees, wherein Rosalind
is so admired?

Me believe it! You should be making sure that the woman you
love believes it – which I think she is more prone to
doing than she would admit. That is one of the
ways in which women trick their own
consciences. But really, are you the man
who is hanging poetry on trees, poetry that talks
of Rosalind so admiringly.

ORLANDO

I swear to thee, youth, by the white hand of
Rosalind, I am that he, that unfortunate he.

I swear to you, young man, by the pure white hand
of Rosalind, that I am that unfortunate, sad man.

ROSALIND

But are you so much in love as your rhymes speak?

But are you as in love as you say in your poems?

ORLANDO

A thin chek, which you don't have, a sad eye,

Neither rhyme nor reason can tell how much I

ROSALIND

Love is merely a madness, and, I tell you, deserves
as well a dark house and a whip as madmen do: and
the reason why they are not so punished and cured
is, that the lunacy is so ordinary that the whippers
are in love too. Yet I profess curing it by counsel.

ORLANDO

Did you ever cure any so?

ROSALIND

Yes, one, and in this manner. He was to imagine me
his love, his mistress; and I set him every day to
woo me: at which time would I, being but a moonish
youth, grieve, be effeminate, changeable, longing
and liking, proud, fantastical, apish, shallow,
inconstant, full of tears, full of smiles, for every
passion something and for no passion truly any
thing, as boys and women are for the most part
cattle of this colour; would now like him, now loathe
him; then entertain him, then forswear him; now weep
for him, then spit at him; that I drave my suitor
from his mad humour of love to a living humour of
madness; which was, to forswear the full stream of
the world, and to live in a nook merely monastic.
And thus I cured him; and this way will I take upon
me to wash your liver as clean as a sound sheep's
heart, that there shall not be one spot of love in't.

---

lover her.

*Love is just madness and, truly, deserves
a dark house and a whip, just like insane people do.
The only reason lovers are not punished and then cured
like that is because such insanity of love is so
ordinary that the punishers
are in love, too. Yet I think one needs to cure it
by being counseled.*

Did you ever cure anyone like that?

*Yes, one person, and here is how: I had him imagine that I
was his love and mistress, and every day he had to
woo me. When he did, I acted as a fickle
youth and would cry, act effeminate, change my moods, long for him
and like him, act proud, dream, mock him, be shallow,
inconsistent, full of tears or full of smiles, act
passionate about everything and then about
nothing – as young boys and women are prone
to acting – would like him and then hate
him, would enjoy him and then curse him, would cry
for him and then spit at him, all until I drove the young man
away from this insane love and a toward a living
anger. He then swore off the entire
world and went to live in a monastery.
Thus, I cured him, and in this way I will take the job
of washing your liver as clean as a spotless sheep's
heart, so that not a single spot of love is in it.*

ORLANDO

I would not be cured, youth.

I can't be cured, youth.

ROSALIND

I would cure you, if you would but call me
Rosalind
and come every day to my cote and woo me.

*I can cure you, if you just call me Rosalind
and come every day to my cottage to woo me.*

ORLANDO

Now, by the faith of my love, I will: tell me
where it is.

*I swear by my love I will – tell me
where the cottage is.*

ROSALIND

Go with me to it and I'll show it you and by the
way
you shall tell me where in the forest you live.
Will you go?

*Come with me and I will show you, and on the
way
you can tell me where in the forest you live.
Will you come?*

ORLANDO

With all my heart, good youth.

Will all of my heart, youth.

ROSALIND

Nay you must call me Rosalind. Come, sister,
will you go?

*No, you have to call me Rosalind. Come, sister,
come with us.*

Exeunt

SCENE III. The forest.

Enter TOUCHSTONE and AUDREY; JAQUES behind

TOUCHSTONE

Come apace, good Audrey: I will fetch up your
goats, Audrey. And how, Audrey? am I the man
yet?
doth my simple feature content you?

*Come on, good Audrey. I will fetch your
goats, Audrey. What do you think, Audrey? Am I
the man for you yet?
Do my simple features please you?*

AUDREY

Your features! Lord warrant us! what features!

Your features! God help me! What features?

TOUCHSTONE

I am here with thee and thy goats, as the most
capricious poet, honest Ovid, was among the
Goths.

*I am here with you and your goats, just like
that witty poet, good Ovid, was with the Goths.*

JAQUES

[Aside] O knowledge ill-inhabited, worse than
Jove
in a thatched house!

*Poorly used knowledge is worse that God
kept in a thatched house!*

TOUCHSTONE

When a man's verses cannot be understood, nor
a
man's good wit seconded with the forward child
Understanding, it strikes a man more dead than
a
great reckoning in a little room. Truly, I would
the gods had made thee poetical.

*When a man's poetry is not understood, and
when a man's good jokes are thrown away by
the child named
Understanding, it feels worse than
getting a big bill for staying in a small room.
Truly, I wish
the gods had made you more poetical.*

AUDREY

I do not know what 'poetical' is: is it honest in
deed and word? is it a true thing?

*I don't know what "poetical" means. It is being
honest in action and word? Is it a true thing?*

TOUCHSTONE

No, truly; for the truest poetry is the most
feigning; and lovers are given to poetry, and
what
they swear in poetry may be said as lovers they
do feign.

*No, for the truest poetry often
fakes the most. Lovers tend to use poetry,
and whatever they swear in their poetry is often
exaggerated.*

AUDREY

Do you wish then that the gods had made me

poetical?

TOUCHSTONE
I do, truly; for thou swearest to me thou art
honest: now, if thou wert a poet, I might have
some
hope thou didst feign.

AUDREY
Would you not have me honest?

TOUCHSTONE
No, truly, unless thou wert hard-favoured; for
honesty coupled to beauty is to have honey a
sauce to sugar.

JAQUES
[Aside] A material fool!

AUDREY
Well, I am not fair; and therefore I pray the gods
make me honest.

TOUCHSTONE
Truly, and to cast away honesty upon a foul slut
were to put good meat into an unclean dish.

AUDREY
I am not a slut, though I thank the gods I am
foul.

TOUCHSTONE
Well, praised be the gods for thy foulness!
sluttishness may come hereafter. But be it as it
may
be, I will marry thee, and to that end I have been
with Sir Oliver Martext, the vicar of the next
village, who hath promised to meet me in this
place
of the forest and to couple us.

JAQUES
[Aside] I would fain see this meeting.

AUDREY

And you wish that the gods made me poetical?

I do, yes. Right now you swear to me that you are
honest and chaste – if you were a poet, I could
hope that you are lying.

You don't want me to be chaste?

No, really, unless you were not attractive.
Chastity alongside beauty is like having honey
sweetened by adding sugar.

This fool is logical at least.

Well I am not beautiful, so I pray that the gods
make me chaste.

Yes, but to give chastity to a dirty slut
is like putting good meat on a dirty plate.

I am not a slut, though I am thankful that I am
dirty.

Well God be praised for your dirtiness!
Maybe you will become a slut later. Regardless,
I will marry you, and to do so I have spoken
with Sir Oliver Martext, the vicar in the next
village, who has promised to meet us here
in the forest and marry us.

I won't miss this meeting.

Well, the gods give us joy!

The gods give us joy!

TOUCHSTONE
Amen. A man may, if he were of a fearful heart, stagger in this attempt; for here we have no temple
but the wood, no assembly but horn-beasts. But what
though? Courage! As horns are odious, they are necessary. It is said, 'many a man knows no end of
his goods:' right; many a man has good horns, and
knows no end of them. Well, that is the dowry of
his wife; 'tis none of his own getting. Horns? Even so. Poor men alone? No, no; the noblest deer
hath them as huge as the rascal. Is the single man
therefore blessed? No: as a walled town is more worthier than a village, so is the forehead of a married man more honourable than the bare brow of a
bachelor; and by how much defence is better than no
skill, by so much is a horn more precious than to want. Here comes Sir Oliver.

Amen. A man, if he is scared,
might pause in this attempt – after all, there is no church
in the forest, no congregation except for horned beasts. But what
of it? I will be brave! As awful as horns are, they are also necessary. It is said, "Many men do not know how much
they have." Exactly: many men have horns on their cheating wives,
and they do not know it. Well, that is the proper gift
a wife brings; it's not something he gets himself. Horns? Fine. And are they only for poor men? No, the noblest man
has them as much as the poor rascal does. So is the single man blessed? No, just as a fortified city is more valuable than a village, so too is the forehead of a married man more honorable than the bare brow of a
bachelor. Similarly, it is better to know how to defend oneself rather
than to have no fighting skills at all – so it is more valuable to risk being cheated on than to not be married. Here comes Sir Oliver.

Enter SIR OLIVER MARTEXT

Sir Oliver Martext, you are well met: will you dispatch us here under this tree, or shall we go with you to your chapel?

Greetings Sir Oliver Martext: will you wed us here under the tree, or shall we go with you to your chapel?

SIR OLIVER MARTEXT
Is there none here to give the woman?

And no one here will give the woman away?

TOUCHSTONE
I will not take her on gift of any man.

I will not take her as a gift from someone else.

SIR OLIVER MARTEXT
Truly, she must be given, or the marriage is not lawful.

She must be given or else the marriage won't be lawful.

[Advancing]
Proceed, proceed I'll give her.

Go on, go on: I will give her away.

TOUCHSTONE
Good even, good Master What-ye-call't: how do you,
sir? You are very well met: God 'ild you for your
last company: I am very glad to see you: even a
toy in hand here, sir: nay, pray be covered.

*Good evening, Master Whatever-Your-Name-Is: how are you,
sir? I'm glad you are here, and God bless you for your
company I am quite glad to see you, even though this is a small matter, sir. No, keep your hat on.*

JAQUES
Will you be married, motley?

And you are getting married, fool?

TOUCHSTONE
As the ox hath his bow, sir, the horse his curb and
the falcon her bells, so man hath his desires; and
as pigeons bill, so wedlock would be nibbling.

The ox has his restraints, the horse his bridle, the falcon her bells, so too does the man have his desires. Just like pigeons need a restraint, so wedlock restrains a man.

JAQUES
And will you, being a man of your breeding, be
married under a bush like a beggar? Get you to
church, and have a good priest that can tell you
what marriage is: this fellow will but join you
together as they join wainscot; then one of you will
prove a shrunk panel and, like green timber,
warp, warp.

*And will you, being a man bred nobly, be married under a tree here, like a beggar? Go to a
church and have a good priest who can tell you what marriage is. This fellow will only join you together like a carpenter joins boards. Then one of you will
be a shrunken plank, and, like fresh wood, will warp, and ruin the joining.*

TOUCHSTONE
[Aside] I am not in the mind but I were better to be
married of him than of another: for he is not like
to marry me well; and not being well married, it
will be a good excuse for me hereafter to leave my wife.

*I don't disagree, but I would rather be married by this vicar than someone else – then he is less likely
to marry me well, and if he messes up, then I have a good excuse to leave my wife later.*

JAQUES
Go thou with me, and let me counsel thee.

Come with me and listen to my advice.

TOUCHSTONE
'Come, sweet Audrey:
We must be married, or we must live in bawdry.
Farewell, good Master Oliver: not,--

*Come sweet Audrey,
we must be married or else we live in sin.
Goodbye, Master Oliver, not like I am singing:*

JAQUES

O sweet Oliver,
O brave Oliver,
Leave me not behind thee: but,--
Wind away,
Begone, I say,
I will not to wedding with thee.

O sweet Oliver,
O brave Oliver,
Don't leave me behind you, but
Go away wind,
Go away, I say,
I will not go to marry you.

Exeunt JAQUES, TOUCHSTONE and AUDREY

SIR OLIVER MARTEXT

'Tis no matter: ne'er a fantastical knave of them
all shall flout me out of my calling.

None of that matters: never will the most
dreaming of tricksters
push me out of my calling.

Exit

SCENE IV. The forest.

Enter ROSALIND and CELIA

ROSALIND
Never talk to me; I will weep.

Don't talk to me. I am going to cry.

CELIA
Do, I prithee; but yet have the grace to consider
that tears do not become a man.

*Go on, cry – but you still have to remember
that tears are not very manly.*

ROSALIND
But have I not cause to weep?

Don't I have reason to weep?

CELIA
As good cause as one would desire; therefore
weep.

*As good a reason as you can want, so go ahead
and weep.*

ROSALIND
His very hair is of the dissembling colour.

His hair is red, a lying color, like Judas' hair.

CELIA
Something browner than Judas's marry, his
kisses are
Judas's own children.

*No, it is browner than Judas' hair, but his kisses
are probably similar.*

ROSALIND
I' faith, his hair is of a good colour.

Actually, I think his hair is a very good color.

CELIA
An excellent colour: your chestnut was ever the
only colour.

*Yes, an excellent color, chestnut is a very good
color.*

ROSALIND
And his kissing is as full of sanctity as the touch
of holy bread.

*And his kissing is as holy as touching
the communion bread.*

CELIA
He hath bought a pair of cast lips of Diana: a
nun
of winter's sisterhood kisses not more
religiously;
the very ice of chastity is in them.

*He must have a pair of lips bought from Diana,
the goddess of purity. A nun
of old age does not kiss more religiously than he
does –
they are chaste and cold kisses.*

ROSALIND

But why did he swear he would come this morning, and
comes not?

*Why did he swear to come here this morning, and
then never arrive.*

CELIA

Nay, certainly, there is no truth in him.

Certainly, the is not truthful.

ROSALIND

Do you think so?

Do you really think so?

CELIA

Yes; I think he is not a pick-purse nor a
horse-stealer, but for his verity in love, I do
think him as concave as a covered goblet or a
worm-eaten nut.

*Yes. I think he is not a pickpocket or a
horse thief, but as for his faithfulness in love, I
do think that he is as hollow as a goblet or a
nut hollowed out by worms.*

ROSALIND

Not true in love?

He is not really in love?

CELIA

Yes, when he is in; but I think he is not in.

*Yes, he is when he is – but I don't think he is
actually in love.*

ROSALIND

You have heard him swear downright he was.

But you have heard him swear that he was.

CELIA

'Was' is not 'is:' besides, the oath of a lover is
no stronger than the word of a tapster; they are
both the confirmer of false reckonings. He attends
here in the forest on the duke your father.

*"Was" is different from "is." Besides, the
lover's promises
are no stronger than the tab from a bartender:
they are both confirming a lie. He stays
here in the forest with the duke your father.*

ROSALIND

I met the duke yesterday and had much question with
him: he asked me of what parentage I was; I told
him, of as good as he; so he laughed and let me go.
But what talk we of fathers, when there is such a
man as Orlando?

*I met the duke yesterday and talked to
him for a while. He asked me about my parents
and I said
that they were as good as he is, and he laughed
and let me go.
But why are we talking about fathers when there
is a man like Orlando in the world?*

CELIA

O, that's a brave man! he writes brave verses,
speaks brave words, swears brave oaths and

*O yes, what a brave man! He writes brave
poems,*

breaks
them bravely, quite traverse, athwart the heart of
his lover; as a puisny tilter, that spurs his horse
but on one side, breaks his staff like a noble
goose: but all's brave that youth mounts and
folly
guides. Who comes here?

CORIN
Mistress and master, you have oft inquired
After the shepherd that complain'd of love,
Who you saw sitting by me on the turf,
Praising the proud disdainful shepherdess
That was his mistress.

CELIA
Well, and what of him?

CORIN
If you will see a pageant truly play'd,
Between the pale complexion of true love
And the red glow of scorn and proud disdain,
Go hence a little and I shall conduct you,
If you will mark it.

ROSALIND
O, come, let us remove:
The sight of lovers feedeth those in love.
Bring us to this sight, and you shall say
I'll prove a busy actor in their play.

*speaks brave words, swears brave promises and
breaks them bravely, quickly and across the
heart of his lover. This is just like a cowardly
jouster who rides forward and then breaks his
staff across the other's shield, like a noble
coward. But everyone is brave who is young and
guided by foolishness. Who is coming here?*

Enter CORIN

*Mistress and master, you often asked me
about the shepherd who complains about his
love, whom you saw me sitting with on the
grass, praising the shepherdess who disdains
him proudly, and who was his mistress.*

Yes, what about him?

*If you would like to see a play well-played
between a pale skinned lover
and a glowing, scornful woman,
come with me and I will show you
so you can see it.*

*Come, let us leave here.
Seeing other lovers is good for those in love.
Bring us to see this and you will watch
me become an actor in their play.*

Exeunt

SCENE V. Another part of the forest.

Enter SILVIUS and PHEBE

SILVIUS

Sweet Phebe, do not scorn me; do not, Phebe;
Say that you love me not, but say not so
In bitterness. The common executioner,
Whose heart the accustom'd sight of death
makes hard,
Falls not the axe upon the humbled neck
But first begs pardon: will you sterner be
Than he that dies and lives by bloody drops?

*Sweet Phebe, do not hate me, do not, Phebe.
Say that you don't love me, but don't say it so
bitterly and meanly. The executioner,
whose hard heart is used to the sight of death,
does not immediately swing the ax down on the
bent neck, but first asks to be excused: will you
be more hard-hearted
than he who makes his living by killing others?*

Enter ROSALIND, CELIA, and CORIN, behind

PHEBE

I would not be thy executioner:
I fly thee, for I would not injure thee.
Thou tell'st me there is murder in mine eye:
'Tis pretty, sure, and very probable,
That eyes, that are the frail'st and softest things,
Who shut their coward gates on atomies,
Should be call'd tyrants, butchers, murderers!
Now I do frown on thee with all my heart;
And if mine eyes can wound, now let them kill
thee:
Now counterfeit to swoon; why now fall down;
Or if thou canst not, O, for shame, for shame,
Lie not, to say mine eyes are murderers!
Now show the wound mine eye hath made in
thee:
Scratch thee but with a pin, and there remains
Some scar of it; lean but upon a rush,
The cicatrice and capable impressure
Thy palm some moment keeps; but now mine
eyes,
Which I have darted at thee, hurt thee not,
Nor, I am sure, there is no force in eyes
That can do hurt.

*I don't want to be your executioner:
I'm trying to leave you so I don't hurt you.
You tell me that my eyes look murderous –
what a nice thought, and a probably one,
that eyes, which are so frail and soft,
 which are so cowardly that they shut to keep
dust out,
should be called tyrants, butchers, and
murderers!
With all of my heart, I am frowning at you,
and if my eyes can hurt, then let them now kill
you. Now fake yourself fainting and fall down,
or if you cannot, you shameful man,
then stop lying by saying that my eyes are
murderers!
Now, show me the wound that my eye made in
you. If I scratched you with a pin, there would
be a scar left. If you lean against a rush weed,
a mark from the pressure
is left for a moment on the palm. But my eyes,
which I looked at you with, did not hurt you,
nor is there any ability for eyes
to hurt someone.*

SILVIUS

O dear Phebe,
If ever,--as that ever may be near,--
You meet in some fresh cheek the power of

*My dear Phebe,
If you ever – and hopefully soon –
fall in love with some man's fresh cheek,
fancy,*

86

Then shall you know the wounds invisible
That love's keen arrows make.

PHEBE
But till that time
Come not thou near me: and when that time
comes,
Afflict me with thy mocks, pity me not;
As till that time I shall not pity thee.

ROSALIND
And why, I pray you? Who might be your
mother,
That you insult, exult, and all at once,
Over the wretched? What though you have no
beauty,--
As, by my faith, I see no more in you
Than without candle may go dark to bed--
Must you be therefore proud and pitiless?
Why, what means this? Why do you look on
me?
I see no more in you than in the ordinary
Of nature's sale-work. 'Od's my little life,
I think she means to tangle my eyes too!
No, faith, proud mistress, hope not after it:
'Tis not your inky brows, your black silk hair,
Your bugle eyeballs, nor your cheek of cream,
That can entame my spirits to your worship.
You foolish shepherd, wherefore do you follow
her,
Like foggy south puffing with wind and rain?
You are a thousand times a properer man
Than she a woman: 'tis such fools as you
That makes the world full of ill-favour'd
children:
'Tis not her glass, but you, that flatters her;
And out of you she sees herself more proper
Than any of her lineaments can show her.
But, mistress, know yourself: down on your
knees,
And thank heaven, fasting, for a good man's
love:
For I must tell you friendly in your ear,
Sell when you can: you are not for all markets:
Cry the man mercy; love him; take his offer:

then you will see that the wounds are invisible
when they are made by love's arrows.

But until that time,
do not come near me. And when that time
comes,
mock me mercilessly, without pity,
since I will not pity you until that time.

And why won't you? Please tell me. Who is your
mother
that you insult the injury and exult over causing
it, all at once, that you made on some wretched
man? You already aren't beautiful –
truly, from what I can see in you,
you should go to bed in the dark without a
candle – do you need to be proud and mean as
well? What do you mean by this? Why are you
looking at me?
I don't see anything in you except the ordinary
work of nature. By God,
I think she wants to make me fall in love with
her, too! No, proud woman, do not put your
hope in this: your inky black eyebrows, your
black, silky hair, your eyes calling out to me,
and your milky white cheek do not tame me to
worship you. You foolish shepherd, why are you
following her,
like fog following the wind and rain?
You are a much more proper man
than she is a proper woman: it's fools like you
who by marrying poorly create ugly children.
It's not her mirror, it's you who flatters her,
and from you she sees a better version of herself
than any of her features can.
Mistress, be honest with yourself, bend down on
your knees,
and thank heaven by fasting for giving you a
good man to love you:
I must tell you honestly that
you should sell yourself when you can, because
your price will not always be good.
Give the man mercy, love him, and take his

Foul is most foul, being foul to be a scoffer.
So take her to thee, shepherd: fare you well.

PHEBE
Sweet youth, I pray you, chide a year together:
I had rather hear you chide than this man woo.

ROSALIND
He's fallen in love with your foulness and she'll
fall in love with my anger. If it be so, as fast as
she answers thee with frowning looks, I'll sauce
her
with bitter words. Why look you so upon me?

PHEBE
For no ill will I bear you.

ROSALIND
I pray you, do not fall in love with me,
For I am falser than vows made in wine:
Besides, I like you not. If you will know my
house,
'Tis at the tuft of olives here hard by.
Will you go, sister? Shepherd, ply her hard.
Come, sister. Shepherdess, look on him better,
And be not proud: though all the world could
see,
None could be so abused in sight as he.
Come, to our flock.

PHEBE
Dead Shepherd, now I find thy saw of might,
'Who ever loved that loved not at first sight?'

SILVIUS
Sweet Phebe,--

PHEBE
Ha, what say'st thou, Silvius?

SILVIUS
Sweet Phebe, pity me.

PHEBE

offer. The ugliest combination is to be ugly and scornful, so take her, shepherd, and be well.

Sweet young man, please, rebuke me for a year:I would rather you chide me than this man woo me.

He has fallen in love with you for your meanness [to Silvius] and she is falling in love with my anger. If that is so, then every time she answers you with a mean look, I will be rude with bitter words. Why are you looking at me like that?

I have no ill-will towards you.

*I'm telling you, do not fall in love with me because I am more unfaithful than promises made while drunk.
Besides, I don't like you. If you want to know where I live, it is at the olive trees close by. Come, sister. Shepherd, keep trying on her. Come, sister. Shepherdess, look at him more fondly, and do not be proud. Even if everyone in the world could see, no one has as faulty sight as he does for thinking you beautiful. Come, let's go to the flock.*

Exeunt ROSALIND, CELIA and CORIN

*Dead Shepherd, the poet Marlowe, now I understand your words:
"Who ever loved that loved not at first sight?"*

Sweet Phebe–

What are you saying to me, Silvius?

Sweet Phebe, take pity on me.

Why, I am sorry for thee, gentle Silvius.

I am sorry for you, gentle Silvius.

SILVIUS
Wherever sorrow is, relief would be:
If you do sorrow at my grief in love,
By giving love your sorrow and my grief
Were both extermined.

Wherever there is sorrow, there is relief:
if you are sad that I am sad in my love for you,
you can love me back, and then my sadness and
yours will both be extinguished.

PHEBE
Thou hast my love: is not that neighbourly?

I do love you, as a friend and neighbor.

SILVIUS
I would have you.

I want to have you.

PHEBE
Why, that were covetousness.
Silvius, the time was that I hated thee,
And yet it is not that I bear thee love;
But since that thou canst talk of love so well,
Thy company, which erst was irksome to me,
I will endure, and I'll employ thee too:
But do not look for further recompense
Than thine own gladness that thou art employ'd.

That is just being greedy.
Silvius, there was a time when I hated you,
and I still do not love you,
but since you speak well about love,
your formerly annoying company
I will endure and keep around me in order to
help me. But do not look for anything more
than my own happiness that I can use you.

SILVIUS
So holy and so perfect is my love,
And I in such a poverty of grace,
That I shall think it a most plenteous crop
To glean the broken ears after the man
That the main harvest reaps: loose now and then
A scatter'd smile, and that I'll live upon.

My love is so holy and perfect,
and I am so poorly returned for it,
that I will think of it as an overabundance
just to pick the leftover ears of corn after
someone else reaps the man harvest. Give now
and then a single smile thrown away, and I will
live on that.

PHEBE
Know'st now the youth that spoke to me
erewhile?

Do you know the young man who spoke to me
before?

SILVIUS
Not very well, but I have met him oft;
And he hath bought the cottage and the bounds
That the old carlot once was master of.

Not well, but I have met him often.
He bought the cottage and land
that the old peasant watched over.

PHEBE
Think not I love him, though I ask for him:
'Tis but a peevish boy; yet he talks well;
But what care I for words? yet words do well
When he that speaks them pleases those that

Do not think that I love him, though I am talking
about him. He is an obnoxious boy, but he
speaks well – but why do I care about that? Yet,
words are working well

hear.
It is a pretty youth: not very pretty:
But, sure, he's proud, and yet his pride becomes him:
He'll make a proper man: the best thing in him
Is his complexion; and faster than his tongue
Did make offence his eye did heal it up.
He is not very tall; yet for his years he's tall:
His leg is but so so; and yet 'tis well:
There was a pretty redness in his lip,
A little riper and more lusty red
Than that mix'd in his cheek; 'twas just the difference
Between the constant red and mingled damask.
There be some women, Silvius, had they mark'd him
In parcels as I did, would have gone near
To fall in love with him; but, for my part,
I love him not nor hate him not; and yet
I have more cause to hate him than to love him:
For what had he to do to chide at me?
He said mine eyes were black and my hair black:
And, now I am remember'd, scorn'd at me:
I marvel why I answer'd not again:
But that's all one; omittance is no quittance.
I'll write to him a very taunting letter,
And thou shalt bear it: wilt thou, Silvius?

SILVIUS
Phebe, with all my heart.

PHEBE
I'll write it straight;
The matter's in my head and in my heart:
I will be bitter with him and passing short.
Go with me, Silvius.

when the speaker pleases his audience by them. He is a pretty young man – not that pretty –
but he is proud, and his pride is somehow attractive.
He will become a proper, noble man, and his best feature
is his skin. Just when his tongue offended me, his eyes healed the offense.
He is not very tall, but for his age his is.
His legs are only so-so, but that's fine.
There was a pretty redness to his lips, they were a deeper red color
than that which was in his cheek. It was the difference
between a pure red and a more pink color.
There are some women, Silvius, who, if they saw everything I did, would have gotten close
to falling in love with him. But as for me, I do not love him or hate him, though
I have more reason to hate him than to love him since he did nothing but rebuke me.
He said my eyes and hair were black, and I remember that he scorned me.
I'm surprised I didn't fight back, but that doesn't matter, to say nothing is not just to quit.
I will write him a letter to taunt him and you will take it to him – will you Silvius?

With all of my heart, Phebe.

I will write it now, since the matter is fresh in my head and heart.
I will be mean and short with him.
Come with me, Silvius.

Exeunt

Act IV

SCENE I. The forest.

Enter ROSALIND, CELIA, and JAQUES

JAQUES
I prithee, pretty youth, let me be better acquainted
with thee.

Please, good youth, let me know you better.

ROSALIND
They say you are a melancholy fellow.

They say you are a sad fellow.

JAQUES
I am so; I do love it better than laughing.

I am – I love being sad more than laughing.

ROSALIND
Those that are in extremity of either are abominable
fellows and betray themselves to every modern censure worse than drunkards.

Those who are at the extremes of either are awful
men who open themselves up to every ridicule more than drunkards do.

JAQUES
Why, 'tis good to be sad and say nothing.

But it is good to be sad and not say anything about it.

ROSALIND
Why then, 'tis good to be a post.

Then it is just as good to be a post.

JAQUES
I have neither the scholar's melancholy, which is emulation, nor the musician's, which is fantastical,
nor the courtier's, which is proud, nor the soldier's, which is ambitious, nor the lawyer's, which is politic, nor the lady's, which is nice, nor
the lover's, which is all these: but it is a melancholy of mine own, compounded of many simples,
extracted from many objects, and indeed the sundry's
contemplation of my travels, in which my often rumination wraps me in a most humorous sadness.

I do not have the seriousness a scholar does, which is meant to impress, or the musician's, which comes from fantasy,
nor the court member's, which is a proud seriousness, nor the
soldier's, which comes from ambition, nor the lawyer's,
which is political, nor the lady's, which is polite, nor the lover's, which is all of these things.
My sadness is my own, made from many little things,
taken from many objects, and all of the many things I have traveled to see. When
I think of these things, it wraps me up in a moody sadness.

ROSALIND

A traveller! By my faith, you have great reason to

be sad: I fear you have sold your own lands to see

other men's; then, to have seen much and to have

nothing, is to have rich eyes and poor hands.

JAQUES

Yes, I have gained my experience.

ROSALIND

And your experience makes you sad: I had rather have

a fool to make me merry than experience to make me

sad; and to travel for it too!

ORLANDO

Good day and happiness, dear Rosalind!

JAQUES

Nay, then, God be wi' you, an you talk in blank verse.

ROSALIND

Farewell, Monsieur Traveller: look you lisp and wear strange suits, disable all the benefits of your

own country, be out of love with your nativity and

almost chide God for making you that countenance you

are, or I will scarce think you have swam in a gondola. Why, how now, Orlando! where have you been

all this while? You a lover! An you serve me such

another trick, never come in my sight more.

ORLANDO

My fair Rosalind, I come within an hour of my promise.

A traveller! Then you have great reason to be sad. I fear that you have sold your own land in order to see other men's, and then, when you have seen a lot and have nothing, you have rich eyes and poor hands.

I have gained a lot from my experience.

And your experience has made you sad. I would rather have a clown make me happy than experience make me sad – and to have to travel for it!

Enter ORLANDO

Good day and happiness to you, dear Rosalind!

No, then, Goodbye if you are going to talk in metered poems.

Exit

Goodbye Monsieur Traveller. Keep your accents and wear foreign clothing, and get rid of all of the rights of your own country. Fall out of love with your native land and almost rebuke God for giving you the skin color and character that you have, or I will not really think that you rode in a Venetian gondola. Hello, Orlando! Where have you been all this time? You call yourself a lover! If you treat me with another trick like this, then do not come here again.

My beautiful Rosalind, I have come within an hour of when I promised.

ROSALIND

Break an hour's promise in love! He that will divide a minute into a thousand parts and break but
a part of the thousandth part of a minute in the affairs of love, it may be said of him that Cupid hath clapped him o' the shoulder, but I'll warrant him heart-whole.

You would break a promise with your love by an hour! Whoever
divides a minute into different parts and then is late by one single part of a minute to meet his love, then I think that Cupid
has made him like the woman, but I doubt he loves her with his whole heart.

ORLANDO

Pardon me, dear Rosalind.

Excuse me, dear Rosalind.

ROSALIND

Nay, an you be so tardy, come no more in my sight: I
had as lief be wooed of a snail.

No, if you are this late again, then do not come in my sight again. I
would rather be wood by a snail.

ORLANDO

Of a snail?

A snail?

ROSALIND

Ay, of a snail; for though he comes slowly, he carries his house on his head; a better jointure, I think, than you make a woman: besides he brings
his destiny with him.

Yes, a snail, because even though he is slow, he carries his house with him: a better gift, I think, than you can give a woman. Besides, he brings
his fate with him.

ORLANDO

What's that?

How so?

ROSALIND

Why, horns, which such as you are fain to be beholding to your wives for: but he comes armed in
his fortune and prevents the slander of his wife.

He brings a cuckold's horns with him, which you men are likely to be
blaming your wife for. But he comes armed with his destiny of cheating, and therefore prevents rumors being sad about his wife.

ORLANDO

Virtue is no horn-maker; and my Rosalind is virtuous.

Virtue does not make a husband become unfaithful, and my Rosalind is virtuous.

ROSALIND

And I am your Rosalind.

And I am your Rosalind.

CELIA

It pleases him to call you so; but he hath a

He likes to call you that, but he has a Rosalind

Rosalind of a better leer than you.

with a better face than you waiting for him.

ROSALIND
Come, woo me, woo me, for now I am in a holiday
humour and like enough to consent. What would you
say to me now, an I were your very very
Rosalind?

*Come now, woo me, for now I am in a happy
mood and will consent to what you want. What would you
sat to me now, if I were your true Rosalind.*

ORLANDO
I would kiss before I spoke.

I would kiss you before I said anything.

ROSALIND
Nay, you were better speak first, and when you were
gravelled for lack of matter, you might take
occasion to kiss. Very good orators, when they are
out, they will spit; and for lovers lacking--God
warn us!--matter, the cleanliest shift is to kiss.

*Now, you would be better off speaking first, and
then when you were
out of things to say, you can
kiss. Good speakers, when they have nothing left
to say, spit, and when lovers run out of words –
God
forbid that happen! – the best thing to do is kiss.*

ORLANDO
How if the kiss be denied?

What if she denies my kiss?

ROSALIND
Then she puts you to entreaty, and there begins
new matter.

*Then she is making you beg, and that is a new
conversation.*

ORLANDO
Who could be out, being before his beloved
mistress?

*Who could run out of words if he was in front of
his beloved?*

ROSALIND
Marry, that should you, if I were your mistress, or
I should think my honesty ranker than my wit.

*If I were your mistress, than you would run out
of words, or else my chastity would be worth
less than my wit.*

ORLANDO
What, of my suit?

And I would be out of my suit?

ROSALIND
Not out of your apparel, and yet out of your suit.
Am not I your Rosalind?

*Not out of your clothes, but yes, out of your
petition to love me. Aren't I your Rosalind?*

ORLANDO

I take some joy to say you are, because I would be
talking of her.

ROSALIND
Well in her person I say I will not have you.

ORLANDO
Then in mine own person I die.

ROSALIND
No, faith, die by attorney. The poor world is
almost six thousand years old, and in all this time
there was not any man died in his own person,
videlicit, in a love-cause. Troilus had his brains
dashed out with a Grecian club; yet he did what he
could to die before, and he is one of the patterns
of love. Leander, he would have lived many a fair
year, though Hero had turned nun, if it had not been
for a hot midsummer night; for, good youth, he went
but forth to wash him in the Hellespont and being
taken with the cramp was drowned and the foolish
coroners of that age found it was 'Hero of Sestos.'
But these are all lies: men have died from time to
time and worms have eaten them, but not for love.

ORLANDO
I would not have my right Rosalind of this mind,
for, I protest, her frown might kill me.

ROSALIND
By this hand, it will not kill a fly. But come, now
I will be your Rosalind in a more coming-on
I enjoy saying that you are, because then it is

I enjoy saying that you are, because then it is like I
am talking to her.

Then pretending I am her, I will say that I do not want you.

Then pretending I am me, I will die.

No, die through something else. The poor world is
almost six thousand years old, and in all of this time
no man died on behalf of himself,
that is, from love. Troilus had his brains
beaten out by a Greek club, yet he tried
to die from love, and he is considered a classic hero
of love. Leander, he would have lived many good
years, though he would have become a nun, if not
for that hot midsummer night when he went
to wash himself in the Hellespont and,
finding himself cramped, drowned. The foolish
coroners then said he was a Hero who died for love,
but these are lies: men have died from time to
time, and worms ate their bodies, and none of it
came from love.

I hope Rosalind does not think like this,
because I think her frowns might truly kill me.

I swear by my hand, they would not kill a fly.
But come on, now
I will be your Rosalind in a more agreeable
state of mind. Ask me what you want, and I will

disposition, and ask me what you will. I will grant it.

grant it.

ORLANDO
Then love me, Rosalind.

Love me, Rosalind.

ROSALIND
Yes, faith, will I, Fridays and Saturdays and all.

Yes, I will: on Fridays and Saturdays and the rest of them.

ORLANDO
And wilt thou have me?

And will you have me?

ROSALIND
Ay, and twenty such.

Yes, and twenty like you.

ORLANDO
What sayest thou?

What do you mean?

ROSALIND
Are you not good?

Are you good?

ORLANDO
I hope so.

I hope so.

ROSALIND
Why then, can one desire too much of a good thing?
Come, sister, you shall be the priest and marry us.
Give me your hand, Orlando. What do you say, sister?

Then can one desire too much of a good thing? Come sister, you will be the priest and marry us. Give me your hand, Orlando. What do you say, sister?

ORLANDO
Pray thee, marry us.

I beg you, marry us.

CELIA
I cannot say the words.

I can't say the words, since I'm not a priest.

ROSALIND
You must begin, 'Will you, Orlando--'

You start with, "Will you, Orlando-"

CELIA
Go to. Will you, Orlando, have to wife this Rosalind?

Stop it. Will you, Orlando, have to wife this Rosalind?

ORLANDO

I will.

I will.

ROSALIND
Ay, but when?

Yes, but when?

ORLANDO
Why now; as fast as she can marry us.

Now, of course, as fast as she can marry us.

ROSALIND
Then you must say 'I take thee, Rosalind, for
wife.'

*Then you must say, "I take you, Rosalind, as my
wife."*

ORLANDO
I take thee, Rosalind, for wife.

I take you, Rosalind, as my wife.

ROSALIND
I might ask you for your commission; but I do
take
thee, Orlando, for my husband: there's a girl
goes
before the priest; and certainly a woman's
thought
runs before her actions.

*I might ask why you should be allowed to take
me, but I do take
you, Orlando, as my husband. There, I went
ahead
of the priest – and certainly a woman's thoughts
run ahead of her actions.*

ORLANDO
So do all thoughts; they are winged.

So do all thoughts, they act like they have wings.

ROSALIND
Now tell me how long you would have her after
you
have possessed her.

*Now tell me how long you would stay with her
after you
possessed her.*

ORLANDO
For ever and a day.

Forever and a day.

ROSALIND
Say 'a day,' without the 'ever.' No, no, Orlando;
men are April when they woo, December when
they wed:
maids are May when they are maids, but the sky
changes when they are wives. I will be more
jealous
of thee than a Barbary cock-pigeon over his hen,
more clamorous than a parrot against rain, more

*You should say "a day" and not the "ever." No,
Orlando, men are like April when they woo, but
their passions cool like December when they
marry. Women are May when they are not
married, but the sky changes above them when
they become wives. I will be more jealous
of your than a wild rooster is over his hen,
more talkative than a parrot talking at the rain,
more fond of new things than an ape, and more*

I will.

new-fangled than an ape, more giddy in my desires
than a monkey: I will weep for nothing, like Diana
in the fountain, and I will do that when you are disposed to be merry; I will laugh like a hyen, and
that when thou art inclined to sleep.

ORLANDO
But will my Rosalind do so?

ROSALIND
By my life, she will do as I do.

ORLANDO
O, but she is wise.

ROSALIND
Or else she could not have the wit to do this: the wiser, the waywarder: make the doors upon a woman's
wit and it will out at the casement; shut that and 'twill out at the key-hole; stop that, 'twill fly with the smoke out at the chimney.

ORLANDO
A man that had a wife with such a wit, he might say
'Wit, whither wilt?'

ROSALIND
Nay, you might keep that cheque for it till you met
your wife's wit going to your neighbour's bed.

ORLANDO
And what wit could wit have to excuse that?

ROSALIND
Marry, to say she came to seek you there. You shall
never take her without her answer, unless you take
her without her tongue. O, that woman that cannot

desirous
than a monkey. I will weep at the slightest things, like Diana
crying at the fountain, and I will do it whenever you
feel particularly happy. I will laugh like a hyena when you are trying to sleep.

Will my Rosalind do this too?

I swear by my life, she will do whatever I do.

But she is also wise.

If she wasn't, then she wouldn't be smart enough to do these things. The wiser a woman is, the wilder. Close doors on a woman's wit and it will fly out the windows. Shut the windows and it will leave through the keyhole. Stop that up and it will fly with the smoke out of the chimney.

A man with a wife like that might wonder, "Wit, where are you going?"

You should keep those questions to yourself until you find out that your wife's wit is going to your neighbor's bed.

What wit could excuse that?

She could say she came to look for you there. You will never see her without an answer ready, unless you take her without a tongue. O, any woman who cannot make her sins her husband's faults should make her fault her husband's occasion, let her never nurse her child herself, for she will breed it like a fool!

ORLANDO
For these two hours, Rosalind, I will leave thee.

ROSALIND
Alas! dear love, I cannot lack thee two hours.

ORLANDO
I must attend the duke at dinner: by two o'clock I
will be with thee again.

ROSALIND
Ay, go your ways, go your ways; I knew what you
would prove: my friends told me as much, and I
thought no less: that flattering tongue of yours
won me: 'tis but one cast away, and so, come,
death! Two o'clock is your hour?

ORLANDO
Ay, sweet Rosalind.

ROSALIND
By my troth, and in good earnest, and so God mend
me, and by all pretty oaths that are not dangerous,
if you break one jot of your promise or come one
minute behind your hour, I will think you the most
pathetical break-promise and the most hollow lover
and the most unworthy of her you call Rosalind that
may be chosen out of the gross band of the
unfaithful: therefore beware my censure and keep
your promise.

ORLANDO

never nurse her child herself, or else she will bring
up foolish children!

Rosalind, I must leave you for two hours.

Oh no! Dear love, I cannot wait for you for two hours.

I must eat dinner with the duke. At two o'clock I will be back.

Fine, go ahead, go on. I knew that you would leave me. My friends told me that, and I didn't think about it. Your flattering tongue won me over, but now I am cast away! Come to me,
death! You will be back at two?

Yes, sweet Rosalind.

Honestly, so God help me,
and by all pretty promises that are not dangerous to make,
if you break one little piece of this promise, or come one minute
after two, I will think that you are the most unfaithful man and hollow lover
and that you are unworthy of the woman you call Rosalind that
can be found anywhere among the bands of unfaithful men. Therefore, beware my scorn and keep
your promise.

With no less religion than if thou wert indeed my
Rosalind: so adieu.

ROSALIND
Well, Time is the old justice that examines all such
offenders, and let Time try: adieu.

CELIA
You have simply misused our sex in your love-prate:
we must have your doublet and hose plucked over your
head, and show the world what the bird hath done to
her own nest.

ROSALIND
O coz, coz, coz, my pretty little coz, that thou
didst know how many fathom deep I am in love! But
it cannot be sounded: my affection hath an unknown
bottom, like the bay of Portugal.

CELIA
Or rather, bottomless, that as fast as you pour
affection in, it runs out.

ROSALIND
No, that same wicked bastard of Venus that was begot
of thought, conceived of spleen and born of madness,
that blind rascally boy that abuses every one's eyes
because his own are out, let him be judge how deep I
am in love. I'll tell thee, Aliena, I cannot be out
of the sight of Orlando: I'll go find a shadow and
sigh till he come.

CELIA
And I'll sleep.

I will keep it as strongly as if you were truly my Rosalind. Goodbye.

Time is the judge who examines all criminals like you, so we will let Time decide. Goodbye.

Exit ORLANDO

You have abused our sex in this talk of love: we should rip off your men's clothing and show the world how you have destroyed your own kind.

O cousin, cousin, cousin, my pretty cousin, if only you knew how deeply I am in love! But I cannot put words to it: my feelings have an unknown depth, like the bay of Portugal.

It might rather be bottomless, since as fast as your pour your affection in, it runs out the bottom.

No, that wicked bastard child of Venus who was born from thought and anger and madness, Cupid himself, that blind rascal who plays with everyone else's eyes since his own are blind, let him judge how deeply I am in love. I will tell you, Aliena, I can't stand not seeing Orlando. I will find some shade and sigh until he returns.

And I will sleep.

Exeunt

SCENE II. The forest.

JAQUES
Which is he that killed the deer?

Who killed the deer?

A Lord
Sir, it was I.

It was me, sir.

JAQUES
Let's present him to the duke, like a Roman
conqueror; and it would do well to set the deer's
horns upon his head, for a branch of victory.
Have
you no song, forester, for this purpose?

*Let's show him off to the duke like a Roman
conqueror. And we can put the deer's
horns on his head, like a branch of victory.
Don't
you have a song to sing for this, forester?*

Forester
Yes, sir.

Yes, sir.

JAQUES
Sing it: 'tis no matter how it be in tune, so it
make noise enough.

*Then sing it, no matter what the tune is as long
as it is loud enough.*

singing
*What should be given to him who killed the
dear? His leather skin and his horns to wear.
Then sing for him as he goes home.*

What shall he have that kill'd the deer?
His leather skin and horns to wear.
Then sing him home;

The rest shall bear this burden

Take thou no scorn to wear the horn;
It was a crest ere thou wast born:
Thy father's father wore it,
And thy father bore it:
The horn, the horn, the lusty horn
Is not a thing to laugh to scorn.

*Don't be ashamed to wear the horn,
it was worn before you were born:
your father's father wore it,
and your father brought it with him:
the horn, the horn, the good horn,
is not a thing to laugh at and mock.*

Exeunt

SCENE III. The forest.

ROSALIND

How say you now? Is it not past two o'clock?
and
here much Orlando!

*What do you think now? Isn't it past two
o'clock? And
I see Orlando everywhere!*

CELIA

I warrant you, with pure love and troubled brain,
he
hath ta'en his bow and arrows and is gone forth
to
sleep. Look, who comes here.

*I bet that with his pure love and worried mind,
he
took his bow and arrows and went out to
sleep. Look, someone coming.*

Enter SILVIUS

SILVIUS

My errand is to you, fair youth;
My gentle Phebe bid me give you this:
I know not the contents; but, as I guess
By the stern brow and waspish action
Which she did use as she was writing of it,
It bears an angry tenor: pardon me:
I am but as a guiltless messenger.

*Pretty youth, I have been tasked to find you:
my gentle Phebe asked me to give you this.
I don't know the contents, but I would guess,
from the stern forehead and her wasplike
movements that she had while writing it,
that it is an angry letter. Excuse me from this,
I am a blameless messenger.*

ROSALIND

Patience herself would startle at this letter
And play the swaggerer; bear this, bear all:
She says I am not fair, that I lack manners;
She calls me proud, and that she could not love
me,
Were man as rare as phoenix. 'Od's my will!
Her love is not the hare that I do hunt:
Why writes she so to me? Well, shepherd, well,
This is a letter of your own device.

*Patience herself would be startled reading this
letter,
and would fight back. I must bear it all:
she says I am not attractive, that I lack manners,
that I am proud, and that she would not love me
even if men were as rare as phoenix birds. By
God! I am not hunting after her love,
why does she write this to me? Shepherd,
I think you wrote this letter.*

SILVIUS

No, I protest, I know not the contents:
Phebe did write it.

*No, honestly. I don't know what it says;
Phebe wrote it.*

ROSALIND

Come, come, you are a fool
And turn'd into the extremity of love.
I saw her hand: she has a leathern hand.

*Come on, you are a fool
and have done extreme things because of love.
I saw her hand, she has a rough hand,*

A freestone-colour'd hand; I verily did think
That her old gloves were on, but 'twas her hands:
She has a huswife's hand; but that's no matter:
I say she never did invent this letter;
This is a man's invention and his hand.

SILVIUS
Sure, it is hers.

ROSALIND
Why, 'tis a boisterous and a cruel style.
A style for-challengers; why, she defies me,
Like Turk to Christian: women's gentle brain
Could not drop forth such giant-rude invention,
Such Ethiope words, blacker in their effect
Than in their countenance. Will you hear the letter?

SILVIUS
So please you, for I never heard it yet;
Yet heard too much of Phebe's cruelty.

ROSALIND
She Phebes me: mark how the tyrant writes.

Art thou god to shepherd turn'd,
That a maiden's heart hath burn'd?
Can a woman rail thus?

SILVIUS
Call you this railing?

ROSALIND
[Reads]
Why, thy godhead laid apart,
Warr'st thou with a woman's heart?
Did you ever hear such railing?
Whiles the eye of man did woo me,
That could do no vengeance to me.
Meaning me a beast.
If the scorn of your bright eyne
Have power to raise such love in mine,

*brown in color – in fact I thought
that she was wearing gloves, but they were her hands.
She has housewife's hands, but that doesn't matter: I say she never wrote this letter,
and that it is the invention of a man and his hand.*

Certainly it is hers.

*It is written in such a boisterous and cruel style
– like she wants a challenger. She challenges me
like a Turk does a Christian. A woman's gentle brain
could not have dropped such rude words,
such black words, blacker in meaning
than in their words even. Will you hear it?*

*If you would like; I haven't heard it yet,
though I have heard a lot of Phebe's cruelty.*

She acts like herself to me, now. Listen how she writes.

Reads

*"Are you a god turned into a shepherd,
that you know how to burn my heart?"
Can a woman rail like this?*

You think this is railing?

*"Why have you set aside your divinity
in order to war with a woman's heart?"
Have you heard such railing?
"When the eyes of other men wooed me,
they did nothing to hurt me."
Meaning I am a beast.
"If the scorn coming from your bright eyes
has the power to make me feel love,*

Alack, in me what strange effect
Would they work in mild aspect!
Whiles you chid me, I did love;
How then might your prayers move!
He that brings this love to thee
Little knows this love in me:
And by him seal up thy mind;
Whether that thy youth and kind
Will the faithful offer take
Of me and all that I can make;
Or else by him my love deny,
And then I'll study how to die.

then what awful effects
would come from you looking kindly at me!
While you rebuke me, I love you –
how much more powerfully would your prayers
move me! He that brings this love letter to you
does not know of my love for you
so send your reply by him.
Tell me whether your youth and beauty
can take my faithful offer
giving you me and everything I can,
or else tell him that you deny my love
so that I can prepare to die."

SILVIUS
Call you this chiding?

You call this a cruel letter?

CELIA
Alas, poor shepherd!

How saw, poor shepherd!

ROSALIND
Do you pity him? no, he deserves no pity. Wilt
thou love such a woman? What, to make thee an
instrument and play false strains upon thee! not
to
be endured! Well, go your way to her, for I see
love hath made thee a tame snake, and say this
to
her: that if she love me, I charge her to love
thee; if she will not, I will never have her unless
thou entreat for her. If you be a true lover,
hence, and not a word; for here comes more
company.

You pity him? He does not deserve pity. Why
would you love such a woman? In order to make
you into an instrument so she can play her own
songs on you? That should not
be endured! Go back to her, for I see
that your love has made you into her own tame
pet, and tell her: if she loves me, then I say she
should love you. If she will not love you, then I
will never have her unless
you beg me to take her. If you are a true lover
then go without speaking. More people are
coming.

Exit SILVIUS

Enter OLIVER

OLIVER
Good morrow, fair ones: pray you, if you know,
Where in the purlieus of this forest stands
A sheep-cote fenced about with olive trees?

Good morning, pretty ones. Can you tell me, if
you know, where in this forest stands
a shepherd's cottage, fenced with olive trees?

CELIA
West of this place, down in the neighbour
bottom:
The rank of osiers by the murmuring stream

It is west of this place, down in the next valley.
The willows by the murmuring stream
on your right will take you to the house.

Left on your right hand brings you to the place.
But at this hour the house doth keep itself;
There's none within.

At this time, though, the house is empty and no one is there.

OLIVER
If that an eye may profit by a tongue,
Then should I know you by description;
Such garments and such years: 'The boy is fair,
Of female favour, and bestows himself
Like a ripe sister: the woman low
And browner than her brother.' Are not you
The owner of the house I did inquire for?

If seeing something can be aided by hearing something, then I think I know you from a description I heard of your clothes and years: "The boy is pretty, like a woman, and carries himself like a mature sister: the woman is shorter and darker than her brother." Aren't you the owners of the house I am asking about?

CELIA
It is no boast, being ask'd, to say we are.

Since you ask, it is not boasting to say that we are.

OLIVER
Orlando doth commend him to you both,
And to that youth he calls his Rosalind
He sends this bloody napkin. Are you he?

Orland sends his regards to you both and to whomever he calls Rosalind, he sends this bloody handkerchief. Are you him?

ROSALIND
I am: what must we understand by this?

I am, what does this mean?

OLIVER
Some of my shame; if you will know of me
What man I am, and how, and why, and where
This handkercher was stain'd.

It means some shame of mine, if you will listen to me say who I am, and how, and why, and where this handkerchief was stained.

CELIA
I pray you, tell it.

Please, tell us.

OLIVER
When last the young Orlando parted from you
He left a promise to return again
Within an hour, and pacing through the forest,
Chewing the food of sweet and bitter fancy,
Lo, what befell! he threw his eye aside,
And mark what object did present itself:
Under an oak, whose boughs were moss'd with age
And high top bald with dry antiquity,
A wretched ragged man, o'ergrown with hair,
Lay sleeping on his back: about his neck
A green and gilded snake had wreathed itself,
Who with her head nimble in threats approach'd

When Orlando last left you, he promised to return in an hour, and, walking through the forest, thinking through sweet and bitter thoughts of love, what happened! He looked aside and saw a certain object: underneath an oak tree, whose boughs were covered with moss, and whose top branches were old from age, a wretchedly ragged man, with hair grown out and unkempt, was sleeping on his back. Around his neck a green and gold snake had wound itself and with her nimble head, she threatened

The opening of his mouth; but suddenly,
Seeing Orlando, it unlink'd itself,
And with indented glides did slip away
Into a bush: under which bush's shade
A lioness, with udders all drawn dry,
Lay couching, head on ground, with catlike watch,
When that the sleeping man should stir; for 'tis
The royal disposition of that beast
To prey on nothing that doth seem as dead:
This seen, Orlando did approach the man
And found it was his brother, his elder brother.

*him by moving towards his open mouth. All of a
sudden it saw Orlando and unwound itself,
gliding away into the bushes. But under that
bush's shade a lioness, its udders dry from
nearby lion cubs, was resting with its head on
the ground, watching closely
to see if the resting man would move – it is
the royal character of the lion
to prey on nothing that looks dead.
Orlando saw the lioness and approached the man,
discovering that it was his older brother.*

CELIA
O, I have heard him speak of that same brother;
And he did render him the most unnatural
That lived amongst men.

*He has spoken of that brother,
whom he described as the most inhumane man
who lived among men.*

OLIVER
And well he might so do,
For well I know he was unnatural.

*He was right to do so,
since I know just how inhumane he was.*

ROSALIND
But, to Orlando: did he leave him there,
Food to the suck'd and hungry lioness?

*But as for Orlando: did he leave him there
to be food for the cubs and the lioness?*

OLIVER
Twice did he turn his back and purposed so;
But kindness, nobler ever than revenge,
And nature, stronger than his just occasion,
Made him give battle to the lioness,
Who quickly fell before him: in which hurtling
From miserable slumber I awaked.

*He turned away twice with the goal of doing
that, but his kindness was more noble than
revenge, and his nature was stronger than his
justice, so he fought the lioness
who quickly fell in front of him: and in that
noise I woke from my miserable slumber.*

CELIA
Are you his brother?

Are you his brother?

ROSALIND
Wast you he rescued?

Were you rescued?

CELIA
Was't you that did so oft contrive to kill him?

Was it you who tried to kill him so often?

OLIVER
'Twas I; but 'tis not I I do not shame

It was I, but it is not still I. I am not ashamed

To tell you what I was, since my conversion
So sweetly tastes, being the thing I am.

ROSALIND
But, for the bloody napkin?

OLIVER
By and by.
When from the first to last betwixt us two
Tears our recountments had most kindly bathed,
As how I came into that desert place:--
In brief, he led me to the gentle duke,
Who gave me fresh array and entertainment,
Committing me unto my brother's love;
Who led me instantly unto his cave,
There stripp'd himself, and here upon his arm
The lioness had torn some flesh away,
Which all this while had bled; and now he fainted
And cried, in fainting, upon Rosalind.
Brief, I recover'd him, bound up his wound;
And, after some small space, being strong at heart,
He sent me hither, stranger as I am,
To tell this story, that you might excuse
His broken promise, and to give this napkin
Dyed in his blood unto the shepherd youth
That he in sport doth call his Rosalind.

CELIA
Why, how now, Ganymede! sweet Ganymede!

OLIVER
Many will swoon when they do look on blood.

CELIA
There is more in it. Cousin Ganymede!

OLIVER
Look, he recovers.

ROSALIND
I would I were at home.

CELIA

---

to tell you who I was, since I have converted,
which tastes much better, to the thing I am now.

And what about the bloody handkerchief?

I'm getting there.
When we told each other what had happened
between us,
we cried over our stories,
like how I came to this deserted place.
Then he led me to the gentle duke here,
who gave me fresh clothing and food,
and committed me to my brother's love.
Orland led me to his cave,
and took off his shirt, and here on the arm
the lioness had torn some flesh away,
which was bleeding all the while. He fainted
and cried as he fainted, "Rosalind!"
I helped him and bound his wound,
and after a little time, since he is a strong man,
he sent me here, since I am a stranger,
to tell you the story so that you can excuse
his absence and broken promise. And he asked
me to give this handkerchief
that was dyed in his blood to the young
shepherd he playfully called his Rosalind.

ROSALIND swoons

Oh, Ganymede! Sweet Ganymede!

Many swoon when they look at blood.

There is more to it than that. Cousin Ganymede!

He is coming to.

I wish I was at our home.

We'll lead you thither.
I pray you, will you take him by the arm?

OLIVER
Be of good cheer, youth: you a man! you lack a man's heart.

ROSALIND
I do so, I confess it. Ah, sirrah, a body would think this was well counterfeited! I pray you, tell your brother how well I counterfeited. Heigh-ho!

OLIVER
This was not counterfeit: there is too great testimony in your complexion that it was a passion
of earnest.

ROSALIND
Counterfeit, I assure you.

OLIVER
Well then, take a good heart and counterfeit to be a man.

ROSALIND
So I do: but, i' faith, I should have been a woman by right.

CELIA
Come, you look paler and paler: pray you, draw homewards. Good sir, go with us.

OLIVER
That will I, for I must bear answer back
How you excuse my brother, Rosalind.

ROSALIND
I shall devise something: but, I pray you, commend
my counterfeiting to him. Will you go?

We will take you there.
Please, will you take his arm?

Feel better, youth. Aren't you a man? You lack a man's heart.

I admit that I do. Ah, sir, someone would think that this was well faked though! Please, tell your brother how well I faked fainting. Ha ha!

That was not fake:
your complexion tells too honestly that this passion
was real.

I promise you, it was fake.

Then take heart, and fake being a man.

I am: truly, I should have been born a woman.

Come on, you look paler by the minute. Please, let's go towards home. Good sir, come with us.

I will, for I must bring an answer back to my brother as to if he is excused, Rosalind.

I will come up with something – but please, tell him
how well I faked. Will you come?

Exeunt

Act V

SCENE I. The forest.

Enter TOUCHSTONE and AUDREY

TOUCHSTONE
We shall find a time, Audrey; patience, gentle
Audrey.

We will find a time to marry, Audrey. Be patient,
gentle Audrey.

AUDREY
Faith, the priest was good enough, for all the old
gentleman's saying.

Truly, that priest was good enough, even for all
of that old man's words.

TOUCHSTONE
A most wicked Sir Oliver, Audrey, a most vile
Martext. But, Audrey, there is a youth here in
the
forest lays claim to you.

No, he was a wicked Sir Oliver, and an evil
Martext. But Audrey, there is a youth in the
forest who claims to love you.

AUDREY
Ay, I know who 'tis; he hath no interest in me in
the world: here comes the man you mean.

Yes, I know who it is. He does not interest me in
the whole world. Here comes the man you are
talking about.

TOUCHSTONE
It is meat and drink to me to see a clown: by my
troth, we that have good wits have much to
answer
for; we shall be flouting; we cannot hold.

I love meeting a country clown. Truly,
we who have good wits have much to apologize
for: we will be messing with him, and we can't
help it.

Enter WILLIAM

WILLIAM
Good even, Audrey.

Good evening, Audrey.

AUDREY
God ye good even, William.

Good evening, William.

WILLIAM
And good even to you, sir.

And good evening to you, sir.

TOUCHSTONE
Good even, gentle friend. Cover thy head, cover
thy
head; nay, prithee, be covered. How old are you,
friend?

Good evening, gentle friend. Put a hat on, put a
hat on. No, please, keep it on. How old are you,
friend?

WILLIAM
Five and twenty, sir.

Twenty-five, sir.

TOUCHSTONE
A ripe age. Is thy name William?

A mature age. And your name is William?

WILLIAM
William, sir.

William, sir.

TOUCHSTONE
A fair name. Wast born i' the forest here?

A good name. Were you born in the forest?

WILLIAM
Ay, sir, I thank God.

Yes, sir, thank God.

TOUCHSTONE
'Thank God;' a good answer. Art rich?

"Thank God," a good answer. Are you rich.

WILLIAM
Faith, sir, so so.

Honestly, sir, so-so.

TOUCHSTONE
'So so' is good, very good, very excellent good; and
yet it is not; it is but so so. Art thou wise?

"So-so" is good, very good, very excellently good.
It is not, it is only so-so. Are you wise?

WILLIAM
Ay, sir, I have a pretty wit.

Yes, sir, I have a good wit.

TOUCHSTONE
Why, thou sayest well. I do now remember a saying,
'The fool doth think he is wise, but the wise man
knows himself to be a fool.' The heathen
philosopher, when he had a desire to eat a grape,
would open his lips when he put it into his
mouth;
meaning thereby that grapes were made to eat
and
lips to open. You do love this maid?

You speak well. I remember a saying, "The fool
thinks he is wise, but the wise man
knows that he is a fool." The heathen
philosopher, when he wants to eat a grape,
opens his lips when he put it to his mouth:
meaning that grapes were made to eat, and
lips were made to open. Do you love this girl?

WILLIAM
I do, sir.

I do, sir.

TOUCHSTONE
Give me your hand. Art thou learned?

Give me your hand. Are you educated?

WILLIAM
No, sir.

No, sir.

TOUCHSTONE
Then learn this of me: to have, is to have; for it
is a figure in rhetoric that drink, being poured
out
of a cup into a glass, by filling the one doth
empty
the other; for all your writers do consent that
ipse
is he: now, you are not ipse, for I am he.

Then learn this from me: if you have something,
you have it.
A drink, being poured out
of a cup and into a glass, fills one and empties
the other. All scholars agree that "ipse" is Latin
for "he," but you are not ipse, for I am he.

WILLIAM
Which he, sir?

Which he, sir?

TOUCHSTONE
He, sir, that must marry this woman. Therefore,
you
clown, abandon,--which is in the vulgar leave,--
the
society,--which in the boorish is company,--of
this
female,--which in the common is woman; which
together is, abandon the society of this female,
or,
clown, thou perishest; or, to thy better
understanding, diest; or, to wit I kill thee, make
thee away, translate thy life into death, thy
liberty into bondage: I will deal in poison with
thee, or in bastinado, or in steel; I will bandy
with thee in faction; I will o'errun thee with
policy; I will kill thee a hundred and fifty ways:
therefore tremble and depart.

He, sir, who will marry this woman. Therefore,
you
clown, abandon – or as a commoner would say,
"leave" ° the
society – or as a commoner would say,
"company," – of this
female – or as a commoner would say,
"woman." All
together that is: abandon the society of this
female, or,
clown, you will perish, or in other
words so you understand, die, or, I will kill you,
make you go away, translate your life into your
death, your liberty into imprisonment: I will give
you poison, or beat you with a club, or kill you
with a sword. I will toss you around and overrun
you with my words. I will kill you a hundred and
fifty ways, therefore shake from fear, and leave.

AUDREY
Do, good William.

Do leave, good William.

WILLIAM
God rest you merry, sir.

Goodbye, sir.

Exit

Enter CORIN

CORIN

Our master and mistress seeks you; come, away, away!

TOUCHSTONE
Trip, Audrey! trip, Audrey! I attend, I attend.

The master and mistress have asked you to come away!

Quickly, Audrey, quickly! I am coming.

Exeunt

SCENE II. The forest.

Enter ORLANDO and OLIVER

ORLANDO

Is't possible that on so little acquaintance you should like her? that but seeing you should love her? and loving woo? and, wooing, she should grant? and will you persever to enjoy her?

Is it possible that from knowing her so little you should fall for her, and that you fall in love with her from seeing her? And then woo her, and then have her accept you? And will you really then marry her?

OLIVER

Neither call the giddiness of it in question, the poverty of her, the small acquaintance, my sudden
wooing, nor her sudden consenting; but say with me,
I love Aliena; say with her that she loves me;
consent with both that we may enjoy each other: it
shall be to your good; for my father's house and all
the revenue that was old Sir Rowland's will I estate upon you, and here live and die a shepherd.

*Don't question the foolishness of it, or her poverty, or our little knowing each other, or my quick wooing, or her accepting, but say it along with me:
"I love Aliena." Say with her that she loves me, and consent that we may enjoy each other. It is to your benefit: our father's house and all of Sir Rowland's fortune I leave to you so that I may live and die as a shepherd.*

ORLANDO

You have my consent. Let your wedding be to-morrow:
thither will I invite the duke and all's contented followers. Go you and prepare Aliena; for look you, here comes my Rosalind.

*You have my consent. Let your wedding be tomorrow,
and I will invite the duke and all of his happy followers. Go and get Aliena ready, for look, here comes my Rosalind.*

Enter ROSALIND

ROSALIND

God save you, brother.

God be with you, brother.

OLIVER

And you, fair sister.

And with you, dear sister.

Exit

ROSALIND

O, my dear Orlando, how it grieves me to see thee
wear thy heart in a scarf!

O my Orlando, it saddens me to see you wear your heart in a sling!

ORLANDO

It is my arm.

It is my arm.

ROSALIND

I thought thy heart had been wounded with the claws
of a lion.

I thought your heart was wounded from the lion's claws.

ORLANDO

Wounded it is, but with the eyes of a lady.

It is wounded, but only from a lady's eyes.

ROSALIND

Did your brother tell you how I counterfeited to swoon when he showed me your handkerchief?

Did your brother tell you how I faked to faint when he showed me the bloody handkerchief?

ORLANDO

Ay, and greater wonders than that.

Yes, and more amazing things than that.

ROSALIND

O, I know where you are: nay, 'tis true: there was
never any thing so sudden but the fight of two rams
and Caesar's thrasonical brag of 'I came, saw, and
overcame:' for your brother and my sister no sooner
met but they looked, no sooner looked but they loved, no sooner loved but they sighed, no sooner
sighed but they asked one another the reason, no sooner knew the reason but they sought the remedy;
and in these degrees have they made a pair of stairs
to marriage which they will climb incontinent, or
else be incontinent before marriage: they are in the very wrath of love and they will together; clubs
cannot part them.

*O, I know what you are talking about. It's true, there was
never anything as sudden as their love except the fight of two rams,
nothing as quick as Caesar bragging, "I came, I saw, and
I conquered," for your brother and my sister had just
met when they looked, and when they looked they loved, and when they loved they sighed, and when they sighed they asked each other why, and
when they knew why they looked for a way to fix their pains of love –
and so on until they built by each step a set of stairs
to marriage which they will climb without control, or
else they will be without control before they marry. They are in
the height of passion and they will be together: even sticks cannot separate them.*

ORLANDO

They shall be married to-morrow, and I will bid the
duke to the nuptial. But, O, how bitter a thing it

*They will be married tomorrow, and I will ask the
duke to come to the ceremony. But O, how bitter*

is to look into happiness through another man's
eyes! By so much the more shall I to-morrow be
at
the height of heart-heaviness, by how much I
shall
think my brother happy in having what he
wishes for.

ROSALIND
Why then, to-morrow I cannot serve your turn
for Rosalind?

ORLANDO
I can live no longer by thinking.

ROSALIND
I will weary you then no longer with idle
talking.
Know of me then, for now I speak to some
purpose,
that I know you are a gentleman of good
conceit: I
speak not this that you should bear a good
opinion
of my knowledge, insomuch I say I know you
are;
neither do I labour for a greater esteem than may
in
some little measure draw a belief from you, to
do
yourself good and not to grace me. Believe then,
if
you please, that I can do strange things: I have,
since I was three year old, conversed with a
magician, most profound in his art and yet not
damnable. If you do love Rosalind so near the
heart
as your gesture cries it out, when your brother
marries Aliena, shall you marry her: I know into
what straits of fortune she is driven; and it is
not impossible to me, if it appear not
inconvenient
to you, to set her before your eyes tomorrow
human
as she is and without any danger.

*it is to look at happiness through another man's
eyes! As happy as he will be, I will tomorrow be
that depressed in seeing that
my brother will have everything he desires.*

Tomorrow, can I be your Rosalind again?

I can no longer keep pretending.

*I will not tire you anymore with foolish talk.
Listen now, for I have a purpose for my words
and I know you are a smart man, I
don't say this so that you will think highly
of my knowledge, just because I speak highly of
your knowledge,
and I also do not say this to build a better
reputation
for myself in your mind, but only to do
good for you. Believe me when I say
that I can do strange and magical things. I have
since I was three years old, spoken with a
magician, one very strong in his art and yet not
cursed and damned to hell. If you love Rosalind
as much
as you gesture, then when your brother
marries Aliena, you will marry her. I know
where fortune has taken her, and it is
not impossible for me to get her, if it is not
inconvenient
to you, and put her in front of your eyes
tomorrow as a human
and without any danger.*

ORLANDO
Speakest thou in sober meanings?

Are you speaking honestly and seriously?

ROSALIND
By my life, I do; which I tender dearly, though I say I am a magician. Therefore, put you in your best array: bid your friends; for if you will be married to-morrow, you shall, and to Rosalind, if you will.

I swear by my life, which is worth a lot to me, that I am, even if I say I am a magician. Put on your best clothes and invite your friends, for if you want to be married tomorrow, you will be, and if you want to marry Rosalind, you will.

Enter SILVIUS and PHEBE

Look, here comes a lover of mine and a lover of hers.

Look, here comes one who loves me, and one who loves her.

PHEBE
Youth, you have done me much ungentleness,
To show the letter that I writ to you.

*Youth, it was very unkind
to show him the letter I wrote to you.*

ROSALIND
I care not if I have: it is my study
To seem despiteful and ungentle to you:
You are there followed by a faithful shepherd;
Look upon him, love him; he worships you.

*I don't care that I did. I am trying
to be spiteful and unkind to you.
You are followed by a faithful shepherd,
so look at him and love him: he worships you.*

PHEBE
Good shepherd, tell this youth what 'tis to love.

Good shepherd, tell this youth what it means to love someone.

SILVIUS
It is to be all made of sighs and tears;
And so am I for Phebe.

*It is made of sighing and crying,
and so I am in love with Phebe.*

PHEBE
And I for Ganymede.

And I with Ganymede.

ORLANDO
And I for Rosalind.

And I with Rosalind.

ROSALIND
And I for no woman.

And I with no woman.

SILVIUS
It is to be all made of faith and service;
And so am I for Phebe.

It is to be made of being faithful and one's servant, and I am that for Phebe.

PHEBE

And I for Ganymede.

And I for Ganymede.

ORLANDO
And I for Rosalind.

And I for Rosalind.

ROSALIND
And I for no woman.

And I for no woman.

SILVIUS
It is to be all made of fantasy,
All made of passion and all made of wishes,
All adoration, duty, and observance,
All humbleness, all patience and impatience,
All purity, all trial, all observance;
And so am I for Phebe.

It is to be made of fantasy and daydreams,
made of passion and wishing
all adoration, duty, and devotion,
all humility and patience, and impatience,
all purity, all hardships, all devotion.
And so am I for Phebe.

PHEBE
And so am I for Ganymede.

And so am I for Ganymede.

ORLANDO
And so am I for Rosalind.

And so am I for Rosalind.

ROSALIND
And so am I for no woman.

And so am I for no woman.

PHEBE
If this be so, why blame you me to love you?

If this is true, then why do you blame me for loving you?

SILVIUS
If this be so, why blame you me to love you?

If this is true, then why do you blame me for loving you?

ORLANDO
If this be so, why blame you me to love you?

If this is true, then why do you blame me for loving you?

ROSALIND
Who do you speak to, 'Why blame you me to love you?'

Who are you talking to with this?

ORLANDO
To her that is not here, nor doth not hear.

To her that is not here and does not hear.

ROSALIND
Pray you, no more of this; 'tis like the howling of Irish wolves against the moon.

Please, all of you, stop. It is like Irish wolves howling at the moon.

I will help you, if I can:

To SILVIUS

I will help, if I can.

To PHEBE

I would love you, if I could. To-morrow meet me all together.

If I could, I would love you too. Tomorrow meet me, everyone.

To PHEBE

I will marry you, if ever I marry woman, and I'll be
married to-morrow:

If I ever marry a woman, I will marry you, and I will be
married tomorrow.

To ORLANDO

I will satisfy you, if ever I satisfied man, and you shall be married to-morrow:

I will satisfy you, more than I ever satisfied a man, and you shall be married tomorrow.

To SILVIUS

I will content you, if what pleases you contents you, and you shall be married to-morrow.

You will be happy, if what pleases you makes you happy, and you will be married tomorrow.

To ORLANDO

As you love Rosalind, meet:

Since you love Rosalind, come.

To SILVIUS

as you love Phebe, meet: and as I love no woman,
I'll meet. So fare you well: I have left you commands.

And since you love Phebe, come. And I love no woman,
and will come. Fare you all well, you have my commands for tomorrow.

SILVIUS
I'll not fail, if I live.

As I live, I will be there.

PHEBE
Nor I.

Me too.

ORLANDO
Nor I.

Me too.

Exeunt

SCENE III. The forest.

Enter TOUCHSTONE and AUDREY

TOUCHSTONE
To-morrow is the joyful day, Audrey; to-morrow will
we be married.

*Tomorrow is the happy day, Audrey. Tomorrow we will
be married.*

AUDREY
I do desire it with all my heart; and I hope it is
no dishonest desire to desire to be a woman of the
world. Here comes two of the banished duke's pages.

*I desire it with all of my heart. I hope it is
not unchaste of me to desire to be a married woman.
Here come two of the duke's pages.*

Enter two Pages

First Page
Well met, honest gentleman.

Hello, honest gentlemen.

TOUCHSTONE
By my troth, well met. Come, sit, sit, and a song.

Truly, good to see you. Come and sit, and sing a song.

Second Page
We are for you: sit i' the middle.

We are here for you, sit in the middle.

First Page
Shall we clap into't roundly, without hawking or
spitting or saying we are hoarse, which are the only
prologues to a bad voice?

*Shall we go right into it, without coughing or
spitting or saying we are hoarse, all
excuses to saying we have bad voices?*

Second Page
I'faith, i'faith; and both in a tune, like two
gipsies on a horse.

*Yes, yes, and everyone on the same tune,
together, like two
riders on one horse.*

SONG.
It was a lover and his lass,
With a hey, and a ho, and a hey nonino,
That o'er the green corn-field did pass
In the spring time, the only pretty ring time,
When birds do sing, hey ding a ding, ding:
Sweet lovers love the spring.
Between the acres of the rye,
With a hey, and a ho, and a hey nonino

*A lover and his woman
with a hey, and a ho, and a hey nonino,
walked through a green cornfield
in the spring time, the only good wedding time,
when the birds sing, hey ding a ding, ding:
sweet lovers in the spring.
Between the acres of rye
with a hey, and a ho, and a hey nonino,*

These pretty country folks would lie,
In the spring time, the only pretty ring time,
When birds do sing, hey ding a ding, ding:
Sweet lovers love the spring.
This carol they began that hour,
With a hey, and a ho, and a hey nonino,
How that a life was but a flower
In the spring time, the only pretty ring time,
When birds do sing, hey ding a ding, ding:
Sweet lovers love the spring.
And therefore take the present time,
With a hey, and a ho, and a hey nonino;
For love is crowned with the prime
In the spring time, the only pretty ring time,
When birds do sing, hey ding a ding, ding:
Sweet lovers love the spring.

TOUCHSTONE
Truly, young gentlemen, though there was no great
matter in the ditty, yet the note was very
untuneable.

First Page
You are deceived, sir: we kept time, we lost not
our time.

TOUCHSTONE
By my troth, yes; I count it but time lost to hear
such a foolish song. God be wi' you; and God mend
your voices! Come, Audrey.

those pretty country folk would lie
in the spring time, the only good wedding time,
when the birds sing, hey ding a ding, ding:
sweet lovers in the spring.
They sang a song that hour
with a hey, and a ho, and a hey nonino,
that life is as short as a flower,
in the spring time, the only good wedding time,
when the birds sing, hey ding a ding, ding:
sweet lovers in the spring.
So take the time today
with a hey, and a ho, and a hey nonino,
for love is crowned with as the best,
in the spring time, the only good wedding time,
when the birds sing, hey ding a ding, ding:
sweet lovers in the spring.

Truly, young men, though there wasn't much
difficulty in that little song, still it sounded
completely out of tune.

You are wrong, sir: we kept the song's pace and
didn't lose it.

Truthfully, yes. I count it as lost time when I hear
such a foolish song. Goodbye, and God fix
your voices! Come, Audrey.

Exeunt

SCENE IV. The forest.

Enter DUKE SENIOR, AMIENS, JAQUES, ORLANDO, OLIVER, and CELIA

DUKE SENIOR
Dost thou believe, Orlando, that the boy
Can do all this that he hath promised?

Do you really believe, Orlando, that that boy can do everything he promised?

ORLANDO
I sometimes do believe, and sometimes do not;
As those that fear they hope, and know they
fear.

Sometimes I believe it, and sometimes I do not, like those who are afraid to hope for something, but they know they are afraid.

Enter ROSALIND, SILVIUS, and PHEBE

ROSALIND
Patience once more, whiles our compact is
urged:
You say, if I bring in your Rosalind,
You will bestow her on Orlando here?

Be patient, while I go over our contract. Duke, if I bring your Rosalind, you will give her to Orlando?

DUKE SENIOR
That would I, had I kingdoms to give with her.

Yes, and I would give kingdoms with her if I had any.

ROSALIND
And you say, you will have her, when I bring
her?

And you say that you will marry her if I bring her?

ORLANDO
That would I, were I of all kingdoms king.

I would, even if I were king of every kingdom.

ROSALIND
You say, you'll marry me, if I be willing?

You say that you will marry me if I am willing?

PHEBE
That will I, should I die the hour after.

Yes, or I will die the next hour.

ROSALIND
But if you do refuse to marry me,
You'll give yourself to this most faithful
shepherd?

But if you decide not to marry me, then you will marry this faithful shepherd?

PHEBE
So is the bargain.

That's the agreement.

ROSALIND
You say, that you'll have Phebe, if she will?

And you will have Phebe if she will marry you?

SILVIUS
Though to have her and death were both one
thing.

Even if to marry her was to die.

ROSALIND
I have promised to make all this matter even.
Keep you your word, O duke, to give your
daughter;
You yours, Orlando, to receive his daughter:
Keep your word, Phebe, that you'll marry me,
Or else refusing me, to wed this shepherd:
Keep your word, Silvius, that you'll marry her.
If she refuse me: and from hence I go,
To make these doubts all even.

I have promised to make this all even.
Keep your word, Duke, to give your daughter,
and you yours, Orlando, to receiver her.
Keep your word, Phebe, that you will marry me
or if you decide not to, to marry the shepherd.
Keep your word, Silvius, that you will marry her
if she refuses me. Now I go
to make all of this even.

Exeunt ROSALIND and CELIA

DUKE SENIOR
I do remember in this shepherd boy
Some lively touches of my daughter's favour.

I do see some resemblance in this shepherd boy
to parts of my daughter's appearance.

ORLANDO
My lord, the first time that I ever saw him
Methought he was a brother to your daughter:
But, my good lord, this boy is forest-born,
And hath been tutor'd in the rudiments
Of many desperate studies by his uncle,
Whom he reports to be a great magician,
Obscured in the circle of this forest.

My lord, when I first saw him,
I thought he was a brother to your daughter:
but good lord, this boy was born in the forest
and has been tutored in nobility
through many lessons from his uncle,
whom he says is a great magician
hidden within this forest.

Enter TOUCHSTONE and AUDREY

JAQUES
There is, sure, another flood toward, and these
couples are coming to the ark. Here comes a pair
of
very strange beasts, which in all tongues are
called fools.

There must be another flood coming, with all of
these
couples lining up to enter the ark. Here are two
strange beasts, which must be called fools.

TOUCHSTONE
Salutation and greeting to you all!

Salutations and greetings everyone!

JAQUES
Good my lord, bid him welcome: this is the
motley-minded gentleman that I have so often
met in

Good lord, welcome this man. He is the
court's clown whom I have often met in
the forest: he swears to have been a court

the forest: he hath been a courtier, he swears.

member.

TOUCHSTONE
If any man doubt that, let him put me to my
purgation. I have trod a measure; I have flattered
a lady; I have been politic with my friend,
smooth
with mine enemy; I have undone three tailors; I
have
had four quarrels, and like to have fought one.

If anyone doubts that, let him try me.
I have danced a little, flattered
a woman, have spoken politely with my friends
and smoothly
with my enemy, and I have ruined three tailors. I
have
had four quarrels, and almost one fight.

JAQUES
And how was that ta'en up?

How did you fix that?

TOUCHSTONE
Faith, we met, and found the quarrel was upon
the
seventh cause.

Well we met, and found the quarrel was on the
seventh cause.

JAQUES
How seventh cause? Good my lord, like this
fellow.

The seventh cause? Good lord, do like this man.

DUKE SENIOR
I like him very well.

I like him very well.

TOUCHSTONE
God 'ild you, sir; I desire you of the like. I
press in here, sir, amongst the rest of the country
copulatives, to swear and to forswear: according
as
marriage binds and blood breaks: a poor virgin,
sir, an ill-favoured thing, sir, but mine own; a
poor
humour of mine, sir, to take that that no man
else
will: rich honesty dwells like a miser, sir, in a
poor house; as your pearl in your foul oyster.

God bless you, sir, for I desire the same thing as
the others here. I came among the rest of these
country couples, to swear to one and swear off
others, since marriage binds and breaks apart
blood relatives. This poor virgin,
sir, is an ugly thing, but my ugly thing. It is a
poor
trait of mine, sir, to take what no one else
wants. Her being chaste and ugly is like a rich
man living like a poor man in a poor house, like
a pearl in a disgusting oyster.

DUKE SENIOR
By my faith, he is very swift and sententious.

Truly, he is quick and wise.

TOUCHSTONE
According to the fool's bolt, sir, and such dulcet
diseases.

It's the jester's lightning, quickly gone, to be
diseased this sweetly.

JAQUES
But, for the seventh cause; how did you find the quarrel on the seventh cause?

Back to the seventh cause. What was the quarrel on the seventh cause?

TOUCHSTONE
Upon a lie seven times removed:--bear your body more
seeming, Audrey:--as thus, sir. I did dislike the cut of a certain courtier's beard: he sent me word,
if I said his beard was not cut well, he was in the mind it was: this is called the Retort Courteous. If I sent him word again 'it was not well cut,' he would send me word, he cut it to please himself: this is called the Quip Modest. If again 'it was not well cut,' he disabled my judgment: this is called the Reply Churlish. If again 'it was not well cut,' he would answer, I spake not true: this is called the Reproof Valiant. If again 'it was not well cut,' he would say I lied: this is called the Counter-cheque Quarrelsome: and so to the Lie Circumstantial and the Lie Direct.

Our argument when through seven parts – stand up
straight, Audrey – like this, sir. I disliked the way a certain court member cut his beard. He sent me a word
saying that even if I don't like it, he thinks it is fine: this is called the "Courteous Retort." If I said it again, then he
would say that he cut it just to please himself: that is called the "Modest Quip." If I said it again, that it was not cut well, he would say that my judgment is meaningless: this is called the "Churlish Reply." If I said it again he would just say that it is not true: this is called the "Valiant Reproof." If I said it again he would say that I lied: this is called the "Argumentative Countercheck." And it continued to the "Circumstantial Lie" and the "Direct Lie."

JAQUES
And how oft did you say his beard was not well cut?

How often did you say his beard did not look good?

TOUCHSTONE
I durst go no further than the Lie Circumstantial, nor he durst not give me the Lie Direct; and so we
measured swords and parted.

I would go no further than the "Circumstantial Lie,"
and he would not dare to give me the "Direct Lie," so we
drew swords, and then stopped fighting.

JAQUES
Can you nominate in order now the degrees of the lie?

What were the steps of lying again?

TOUCHSTONE
O sir, we quarrel in print, by the book; as you have
books for good manners: I will name you the degrees.
The first, the Retort Courteous; the second, the Quip Modest; the third, the Reply Churlish; the fourth, the Reproof Valiant; the fifth, the Countercheque Quarrelsome; the sixth, the Lie

Sir, we quarrel by the book, just like there is a book for good manners. I will name you
the degrees. The first is the Courteous Retort, then the
Modest Quip, then the Churlish Reply, the fourth is the Valiant Reproof, the fifth is the Argumentative Countercheck, the sixth is the

with
Circumstance; the seventh, the Lie Direct. All
these you may avoid but the Lie Direct; and you may
avoid that too, with an If. I knew when seven
justices could not take up a quarrel, but when the
parties were met themselves, one of them thought but
of an If, as, 'If you said so, then I said so;' and
they shook hands and swore brothers. Your If is the
only peacemaker; much virtue in If.

Circumstantial Lie, and the seventh is the Direct Lie.
You can avoid all of these, and you can avoid the Direct Lie with a well placed "If." I knew a case that seven judges could not fix, but when the parties themselves met, one of them came up with the If, like, "If you said this, then I said that," and they shook hands and swore that they were brothers. The If is the only real peacemaker. There is much goodness in If.

JAQUES
Is not this a rare fellow, my lord? he's as good at any thing and yet a fool.

Isn't he a rare fellow, my lord? He is talented and wise, but still a clown.

DUKE SENIOR
He uses his folly like a stalking-horse and under the presentation of that he shoots his wit.

He uses his costume and act like a disguise to hide under when he speaks his wit.

Enter HYMEN, ROSALIND, and CELIA Still Music

HYMEN
Then is there mirth in heaven,
When earthly things made even
Atone together.
Good duke, receive thy daughter
Hymen from heaven brought her,
Yea, brought her hither,
That thou mightst join her hand with his
Whose heart within his bosom is.

There is happiness in heaven when earthly things are evened out and put together.
Good duke, receive your daughter whom Hymen brought, yes, brought here so that you can join her hand with his whose heart is hers.

ROSALIND
[To DUKE SENIOR] To you I give myself, for I am yours.

To you I give myself, since I am yours.

To ORLANDO

To you I give myself, for I am yours.

To you I give myself, since I am yours.

DUKE SENIOR
If there be truth in sight, you are my daughter.

If what I see is true, you are my daughter.

ORLANDO

If there be truth in sight, you are my Rosalind.

If what I see is true, you are my Rosalind.

PHEBE
If sight and shape be true,
Why then, my love adieu!

If this sight is true,
then goodbye my love!

ROSALIND
I'll have no father, if you be not he:
I'll have no husband, if you be not he:
Nor ne'er wed woman, if you be not she.

I won't have a father if you are not him,
I won't have a husband if you are not him,
and I won't marry a woman, if you are not her.

HYMEN
Peace, ho! I bar confusion:
'Tis I must make conclusion
Of these most strange events:
Here's eight that must take hands
To join in Hymen's bands,
If truth holds true contents.

Stop now! No confusion necessary,
I will make clear
these strange events.
There are eight here who must take hands
and join in marriage,
if you are all pleased with the truth in front of
you.
[to Orlando and Rosalind]
No trials will part you.

You and you no cross shall part:

You and you are heart in heart

[to Oliver and Celia]
You are joined in your hearts.
[to Phebe}
You must accept his love

You to his love must accord,
Or have a woman to your lord:

or have a woman as your lord.
[to Touchstone and Audrey]
You two are bound like

You and you are sure together,
As the winter to foul weather.

the winter is to bad weather.
[to all]

Whiles a wedlock-hymn we sing,
Feed yourselves with questioning;
That reason wonder may diminish,
How thus we met, and these things finish.

While we sing a wedding song,
take in your questions
so that reason can take away your surprise
at how all of these things happened.

SONG.
Wedding is great Juno's crown:
O blessed bond of board and bed!
'Tis Hymen peoples every town;
High wedlock then be honoured:
Honour, high honour and renown,
To Hymen, god of every town!

Wedding is the crown of God,
O blessed bond of the home-life!
It is I who makes people for every town,
so marriage should be honored.
Honor, high honor, and renown,
to Hymen, the god of every town!

DUKE SENIOR
O my dear niece, welcome thou art to me!
Even daughter, welcome, in no less degree.

My niece, you are welcome here!
Even welcome as a true daughter to me.

PHEBE
I will not eat my word, now thou art mine;
Thy faith my fancy to thee doth combine.

I won't break my word: you are mine.
Your faith has made me fancy you.

Enter JAQUES DE BOYS

JAQUES DE BOYS
Let me have audience for a word or two:
I am the second son of old Sir Rowland,
That bring these tidings to this fair assembly.
Duke Frederick, hearing how that every day
Men of great worth resorted to this forest,
Address'd a mighty power; which were on foot,
In his own conduct, purposely to take
His brother here and put him to the sword:
And to the skirts of this wild wood he came;
Where meeting with an old religious man,
After some question with him, was converted
Both from his enterprise and from the world,
His crown bequeathing to his banish'd brother,
And all their lands restored to them again
That were with him exiled. This to be true,
I do engage my life.

Everyone, give me your attention for a word.
I am the second son of Sir Rowland,
and I bring news to this congregation.
Duke Frederick, when he heard that every day
more noble and strong men were coming to this
forest, gathered a large army, which were
marching at his word to fight against
his brother and kill him with the sword.
At the edge of the forest, he met an old religious
man who spoke with him, and then the Duke was
converted, and gave up his mission, even
retreating from the world.
He has left his crown to his banished brother,
and restored the lands of the exiles
to all of them that were forced out. This is true,
I swear by my life.

DUKE SENIOR
Welcome, young man;
Thou offer'st fairly to thy brothers' wedding:
To one his lands withheld, and to the other
A land itself at large, a potent dukedom.
First, in this forest, let us do those ends
That here were well begun and well begot:
And after, every of this happy number
That have endured shrewd days and nights with us
Shall share the good of our returned fortune,
According to the measure of their states.
Meantime, forget this new-fall'n dignity
And fall into our rustic revelry.
Play, music! And you, brides and bridegrooms all,
With measure heap'd in joy, to the measures fall.

Welcome young man,
you bring a good present to your brothers'
wedding:
to Oliver his withheld lands, and to Orlando
the land itself, the whole dukedom as
inheritance.
First, let us do those things here in the forest
that were started here.
After that, every person of this happy group
who has endured hard days and nights with us
will have a part of our returned fortune,
according to their ranks.
Meanwhile, let's forget this new nobility
and enjoy our country partying.
Music! And you brides and grooms,
with all of your joy, go dance.

JAQUES
Sir, by your patience. If I heard you rightly,
The duke hath put on a religious life
And thrown into neglect the pompous court?

Sire, one moment: if I heard you correctly,
did you say that the duke has taken on a
religious life

JAQUES DE BOYS
He hath.

JAQUES
To him will I : out of these convertites
There is much matter to be heard and learn'd.

You to your former honour I bequeath;
Your patience and your virtue well deserves it:

You to a love that your true faith doth merit:

You to your land and love and great allies:

You to a long and well-deserved bed:

And you to wrangling; for thy loving voyage
Is but for two months victuall'd. So, to your
pleasures:
I am for other than for dancing measures.

DUKE SENIOR
Stay, Jaques, stay.

JAQUES
To see no pastime I what you would have
I'll stay to know at your abandon'd cave.

DUKE SENIOR
Proceed, proceed: we will begin these rites,
As we do trust they'll end, in true delights.

EPILOGUE

and thrown away his courtly nobility?

He has.

*Then I will go to him: these converts
have a lot from which I can hear and learn.*

To DUKE SENIOR

*I leave you with your former title:
your patience and goodness deserve it.*

To ORLANDO

You I leave to a love your faith has earned you.

To OLIVER

You to your land and your love and allies.

To SILVIUS

You to a long and deserved bed with your wife.

To TOUCHSTONE

*And you to your fighting, for your marriage
will last for two months. Now go to your
pleasure
and dance, I must seek other things.*

Stay with us, Jacques.

*I would rather not see such fun, but I will
stay at your cave if you need me.*

Exit

*Let's go on, we will begin this ceremony
the way it should end also: with true happiness.
A dance*

ROSALIND

It is not the fashion to see the lady the epilogue;
but it is no more unhandsome than to see the
lord
the prologue. If it be true that good wine needs
no bush, 'tis true that a good play needs no
epilogue; yet to good wine they do use good
bushes,
and good plays prove the better by the help of
good
epilogues. What a case am I in then, that am
neither a good epilogue nor cannot insinuate
with
you in the behalf of a good play! I am not
furnished like a beggar, therefore to beg will not
become me: my way is to conjure you; and I'll
begin
with the women. I charge you, O women, for the
love
you bear to men, to like as much of this play as
please you: and I charge you, O men, for the
love
you bear to women--as I perceive by your
simpering,
none of you hates them--that between you and
the
women the play may please. If I were a woman I
would kiss as many of you as had beards that
pleased
me, complexions that liked me and breaths that I
defied not: and, I am sure, as many as have good
beards or good faces or sweet breaths will, for
my
kind offer, when I make curtsy, bid me farewell.

*One doesn't usually see a woman in the
epilogue, but it is not worse than seeing a man
give the prologue. If it is true that good wine
does not
need advertised, then it is also true that a good
play does not need
an epilogue. Yet good wine still gets good
advertisements
and good plays often are improved with good
epilogues. This is a strange case, then, since
I neither have a good epilogue nor can suggest
that this was a good play! I am not
dressed like a beggar, so begging would not
be attractive for me. My way is to trick you, and
I will start
with the women. Women, I command you, for
your love
of men, to like as much of this play as you
want. Men, I command you for your love
for women – and I can see by your smiles
that none of you hate them – that the play will
please you as something to share with the
women. If I were a woman I
would kiss all of you who have beards and who
pleased
me, complexions that were attractive, and
breaths that
were not disgusting. And I am sure that all of
you who have good
beards or good faces or sweet breaths will, for
my
offer, applaud me farewell when I curtsy to
leave.*

Exeunt

Made in the USA
Monee, IL
28 January 2023

26359099R00077